Skinsinger: Tales of the Kaltaoven
Heather Rose Jones

I0545013

Cover illustration and design by The Illustrated Page Book Design (https://theillustratedpage.net/design/)

No generative large data models (AI) have been used in the creation of the text or art of this publication. It is prohibited to include the text or cover image as data for training large data models.

ISBN: 978-1-942794-06-6 (ebook)

978-1-942794-07-3 (paperback)

Published in the United States of America

Table of Contents

Publication History

Skins

The ground raced by under our feet, damp and rotten with last year's leaf-litter. The trees crowded closely overhead, blocking the moonlight. It was so dark that even with wolf-eyes I could barely follow the path. And with the other senses parceled out to the boys... I didn't miss the scents, but the dead-silence made everything unreal to me.

"Dyoan, what do you hear?" I could feel him struggling to put things into words. Words were necessary even when we shared a body like this.

"Only two riders...far behind...fallen back."

I swiveled our ears. "And ahead?"

"Nothing...wait! To the right." I turned our head momentarily to focus. "They've circled around! Laaki, run!"

"Wait. Ale'en, that's upwind. What do you smell?"

His thoughts wailed at me. "I want out! Laaki, let me out!"

I prayed for patience. He was only seven—too young to have the discipline to be carried senseless inside, but it wasn't much easier to be limited to smells. "Soon. Shall we be caught because you're such a baby? Now tell me, what do you smell?"

"Horses. Horses and men. They're sweating a lot."

"No dogs?"

"No. Laaki, let me out!"

"Be still!"

Dyoan leapt to his brother's defense, as usual. "You let him be! It's easy for you."

Easy for me. Those were the words that had gotten us into this.

We were in the kitchen-yard of the White Swan, then; I fetching water from the well and Dyoan sneaking a break from cleaning tables. Now, I've never minded hard, honest work, and we were lucky that Ercin would take on strangers like he did. But Dyoan thought it all beneath us somehow, and the customers could tell and sometimes couldn't resist poking at his touchy pride.

"I want my skin-song! Now!" he said, as if I could produce it at will.

"You'll have it when I've made it, and not before. And if you don't let me do my chores, I won't have time to work on it at all tonight."

"You haven't worked on it for months."

And he was right. But then it was months since I'd had a day to myself, to go off in the woods with the wolf-skin he had inherited from his mother and think wolfish thoughts and craft wolfish rhymes. Our kind are few enough as it is, and fewer still of us have the talent for making the songs that bind skin to man. It was not an easy task and I was not as skilled at it as I'd let them think.

Three months it had been since their father left these two in my care, then wrapped himself in his eagle-skin to confront some nameless stalker. We are often hunted. He never returned, and I was left with an angry youth who had not yet learned to wear his mother's wolf-skin, and a child who had not even that much.

We were chance-met, that small family and I. They barely keeping ahead of their hunters and I seeking more of our kin to give me a place and a purpose. If we'd had time, their father might have bargained with me to craft them songs. Instead he snatched at my promise to see the boys cloaked if he failed. Then he went to hunt the hunter. Three months should have been enough time to have them both wearing skins. But here I was: father and mother and skin-singer, all three, still on the run and hoping the hunters had lost the trail. Three years might not be enough unless we found rest and safety. But there was one thing I could give him now.

"Would you like to go hunting? I can give Ercin some excuse."

He looked at me as if I had offered a starving man a sugared violet. "I want my *skin*! It's easy for you! All you do is throw it over me and say, 'Wear thy skin.' and you think that's the same. It's not the same when I have to come whining back and wait for you to take it off me. You have your feathers—you can't understand."

But I did. And the thought of how lost I would be without my owl-skin was a cold place in my soul. How could he have patience? He was fifteen years old.

He took my silence for something else and had opened his mouth to continue when a sound in the main yard made us freeze. Dyoan turned pale knowing he had broken the rule, talking of skins where someone could hear.

There was silence, then a horse stamped and snorted and a low voice called, "Halloo." A customer then. Dyoan was also part-time stable boy. He sighed and slipped through the gate to the main courtyard.

I would have dropped the matter entirely from my mind if not for the way the new customer stared when I brought his food. Not that I wasn't used to rude stares from some of the men. I schooled myself to a bland look and was relieved when he examined Ercin just as closely later on. Maybe it was just his way.

The inn was busy enough that I didn't track comings and goings. Besides the trade into Karskar, there was the market serving the string of villages all along the valley. So I didn't think of the stranger again until the end of one evening, when the kitchen fires had been banked and the customers had all gone to their beds.

Ercin pulled me aside. "That fellow—the one with the red boots. He was asking questions about you and your brothers." (They weren't my brothers, of course, but it was the simplest explanation.) "Like, where you were from, and did I know your folks, and how long had you been here. You haven't run away from something have you?"

It was a reasonable guess, although runaway bondsmen usually headed for a town. "No, I told you true. We're freeborn, just lost our land."

"He asked something funny, too: did you have a cloak of fur or feathers."

My mind raced to the skins, hidden carefully under our sleeping pallets.

"Now fur I can understand—wouldn't mind one myself when winter sets in—but what would anyone want with a cloak of feathers?"

I shrugged, trying not to shiver. "For pretty, maybe? I heard a story once about a queen with a dress of peacock feathers."

Ercin scratched his head and shrugged in return. "Well, if he bothers you, you let me know. I don't want to lose you."

But I knew then that he would lose us, and soon. We'd been tracked.

I roused the boys from their sleep; Dyoan alert and wary, Ale'en yawning and sleepy-eyed. "We have to leave," I said. "That man was asking questions—the one from the stable. He knows too much." Guilt rose in Dyoan's face with a flush. I stopped a useless apology with a squeeze of his shoulder. "Get your skin, we can't afford to carry anything else."

That wasn't entirely true, for I did fetch our small bag of treasures—the ones we might bargain with if there was no work to offer—along with my owl-skin. I bundled them up and tied it to my belt to ensure it came with us in the change. We'd use the wolf-skin. Owls were not made for long travel.

We slipped out the back, through the kitchen court and over the garden wall. I thought we would be free and safe, but someone must have been watching for us. There was a muffled whinny from the roadway and an answering one. Who were the others? He'd come in alone. Had he hired other travelers for his hunt?

There was no time to wonder. I shook out the wolf-skin and flung it around us as the boys pressed close to my sides. This was different from using a skin-song. This was the rough, crude magic a singer could use in emergencies, forcing a shape on a body, willing or unwilling. "Wear thy skin!" I hissed, and then human speech was ours no more. We would run in one body as a wolf until I chose to release us.

The inn lay in a narrow valley, on the near side of the pass into Ganasset—the better to catch the arriving trade. I might have run for the pass if I thought we could beat the riders. Beyond, the land was thick forest all the way to Karskar. But most of that track was bare ground and there was a moon. Back into the valley lay fields and orchards, thick with farmsteads and watchful dogs. Our best chance was a strip of wooded land along the river. We took to the woods and raced along a deer-path, with the hoof beats of our pursuers falling farther behind. Then we heard other riders flanking us on the road just beyond the fringe of trees.

If I had known the land that lay in this direction better, we might have avoided what came, but when we hunted it had been beyond the pass where we would not disturb the local farmers. So I veered to the left, closer to the river, and didn't notice how the land rose in a steep bank between us and the road. We could have swum the river but I feared it would slow us down too much. Instead we were racing along the narrow track at the base of the rise, up a bit from the water's edge, when the ground crumbled under us and we fell through woven branches into a steep, mud-bottomed pit.

In that first moment of panic I knew we'd been driven deliberately. They'd had days to prepare the pit and I'd foolishly given them the time. Better to have fled that first night.

And here we were, bruised and muddy, with Ale'en shrieking in my mind to be let out, the walls too steep for climbing or jumping, and coming closer, the sound of the hunt. The only escape was up. I drew the wolf-skin off us, bundling it quickly as I shook out the owl cloak.

"Quickly now," I called to the boys, spreading the cloak wide.

Ale'en wailed and scrabbled to the opposite end of the pit. "No! I won't!"

"We have no time for this!" I hissed, reaching for his arm.

But in that moment of confusion Dyoan's instinct was to protect his brother, and he pushed between us saying, "Let him be."

And all that I can offer in my defense is that the hunters were nearly on top of us, there was only one way out, and I had been caged once before.

I wrapped the cloak around me with my skin-song whispering in my mind, clutched the wolf-cloak in my talons, and fled.

Being that I had worn my skin for so long, and that I am a singer, I never needed to voice the song itself to change. But still the echoes of my first creation came back every time I flew.

Time to wear the feathers,
Time to fly the night,
No ground can hold me down now,
No one can stay my flight.

The dark pit shrank beneath me as I tried to stop my ears to the shouts of the hunters and the boys' frightened cries.

Fetch the finely fashioned feather cloak
And clutch it close across me,
Feel the flesh reforming,
Fingers stretching,
Strong and starward striving.

I flew until the weight of the wolf-skin and my own grief bore me down. Then I found a dark place to hide and curled up under the skins, weeping for the trust I had betrayed.

It was two days before I found the courage to return to the pit. The wolf-skin was hidden away safe and I flew unencumbered through the early dusk. The ground around the pit was still churned to mud, but when I followed the hoof marks, they only led me back up around to the road and then disappeared in the mass of tracks. Where had they been taken? Ercin might know, if they had gone that way, but would he tell me? Would he help me at all, knowing now what I am? Better, perhaps, to ask a stranger, who would only be curious in the usual way.

I perched on a milepost, feathers fluffed in indecision, and didn't notice the shadow above me until it slipped steeply through the air. Even then I was frozen a moment in confused recognition, but the intent of the eagle's stoop was unmistakable. I cast forward, hoping to make the shelter of the trees in time. The wind of his turn buffeted me nearly as much as his fisted talons as he knocked me tumbling to the ground. I cast off my feathers, hoping to gain the advantage of size and to no surprise at all, my assailant did likewise.

"Dyoan! What does this mean?" He was not the person I expected to see beneath that eagle-skin.

He folded his arms and smiled smugly. "It means I've found a better singer than you ever were to help us. It only took him half a day to make the skin-song for me and you can't even make one in a month! Now give me back my wolf-skin and go your way."

"He gave you that skin?"

He snarled at me, but I could see the hurt behind it. "What do you care? You left us behind! To die, for all you knew, or worse. Just give me my skin and let us be."

"Dyoan." My voice dropped to a whisper. "The man who chased us wasn't Kaltaoven—wasn't one of us. Who gave you that skin?"

Something in my tone broke through and he looked confused. "He only wanted to help us, you know, but you made us run."

"Dyoan, the last time I saw that skin was on your father."

I watched as he took that in, and the implications crossed his face like scudding clouds. "That doesn't mean... He wouldn't have..."

"How do you know?" I asked harshly. "What do you know of him, except that he collects skins and their wearers? And now he wants you to bring him yours. And mine too, no doubt." I saw that last one hit home. Dyoan might have been content to let me go my way, but I guessed that those hadn't been his instructions.

"He has Ale'en," he said quietly.

I nodded, unsurprised. "Would you lend a skin and not keep something as a pledge?" I thought a moment. "How can I find Ale'en? Will you give me the eagle cloak to go fetch him? I might have a chance to slip in and out if he thinks I'm you."

Dyoan shook his head miserably. "He'll be kept close inside. The singer said he was afraid you would try to steal him."

"And then he'd have no hold on you."

"It didn't sound like that at the time."

But I knew even when I suggested it that running wasn't the answer. There was a man out there who hunted our kind and could sing to our skins as well as we could. I could think of only one way to stop him, and it made me sick with dread. Before I could lose my nerve, I told Dyoan what to do.

He wasn't at the inn but was staying some miles down the valley with one of the farmers there. It seemed he trusted his hosts no more than I would have, for he had arranged to meet Dyoan in a field nearby at moonrise. We glided down to meet him—I hanging limply in Dyoan's talons. The boy shed his skin and stepped away while I made a show of flopping clumsily as I changed, rising unsteadily to one knee.

The stranger came forward, saying, "She wouldn't give it to you then? Just as I said! But we'll get it back—"

At that moment I slipped the owl-cloak from my shoulders and flung it before me like a throw-net crying, "Wear my skin!"

He blinked in surprise—large, golden, owl eyes. I think I held my breath for a full minute waiting for him to realize what had happened. Then with a cry he fled on soundless wings, wearing my feathers to the end of his days, for *I* would never release him.

Dyoan fetched his brother from the farmhouse and as he brought him back draped the eagle-skin around the child's shoulders. Well then, it should have come to him in the normal course of things. We had been driven away from the road of our fate for a time, but our feet had found it again. The older boy looked up at me with troubled eyes.

"Laaki..."

I felt his sympathy but couldn't face it just yet. "So," I said briskly, "I'll have to get to work, with two new songs to make. Will you lend us all your feathers for a bit, Ale'en? I'd have you carry us, but you don't know where I've left Dyoan's skin and it's a bit dark for your first flying lesson, anyway. We had best be far from here by dawn, I think."

He ran his fingers possessively over the feathers, then grinned shyly and handed me the eagle-cloak.

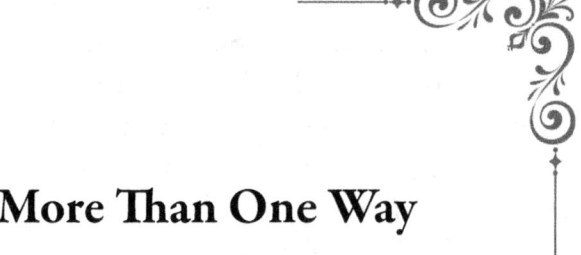

More Than One Way

I waited in the hut most of the night, hoping that I was wrong and that dawn would find me sleepy but undisturbed. There had been murder in Ashóli's eyes when they met mine over her grandmother's grave. I had no intention of stealing the inheritance that she thought hers by right, but I could not tell her so. Not yet. So I waited. Night had always been my element, and though I could no longer use an owl's eyes and ears, there was little danger that she would catch me unaware. No, this night held little danger for me—but for her? Would she pass that threshold and put herself beyond my help?

We had crossed the river around midday two days before—Dyoan and Ale'en and I—and rested a while on a grassy bank overlooking the wide water. Dyoan would have put on his wolf-skin and run ahead exploring, but there were trails and footprints along the shore and I persuaded him to caution.

After we'd crossed, I felt a weight drop away. Ganasset was well and truly behind us now; a land too uncomfortable with what they considered magic to have made *us* comfortable there. I watched Ale'en dancing in the sunlight with his cloak of eagle feathers floating out behind him. He was delighted at having borne us across the water, as only a child can be at having done a grown-up task. He had his skin-song now, and though I was the one who had sung his eagle-cloak around all three of us, it had been his wings that carried us, and his generosity that brought us across dry and safe.

It was hard not to presume upon that generosity, after the long time when neither of them could wear their own skins except by my word. After our narrow escape the year before, I had set all my skills to crafting skin-songs for the two of them. Now that they could sing their own shapes into fur and feathers and back again, I kept my tongue behind my teeth and did not order that part of their lives. But, oh, it was hard, now that I was the slowest one, walking only on two legs. Singing an old skin to a new wearer was hard enough for me. I hadn't yet started the task of crafting a new cloak of my own, not when all our thoughts were for safety and surviving. We hadn't dared to stop long in human settlements in our flight, and living as if we were beasts wore hard on me.

From this side of the river an open woodland rose slowly toward mountains. I squinted into the distance looking for signs of habitation. The rumors behind us said that our people were known here, and I hoped to find a family that would take the boys in. But in a land frequented by Kaltaoven, strangers could as easily be kin or enemies. We are not always comfortable neighbors.

A thread of smoke lifted from behind a hill in the distance and farther up the riverbank a narrow path led in the same direction. We steered our steps toward the smoke. Likely it would be no more than a charcoal-burner's hut or perhaps a hunting camp. We could ask careful questions to guide our quest. Hope was too painful.

They found us first: a woman flanked by two snarling hounds who stepped onto the path before us with no chance for us to hide our strangeness. Dyoan stiffened beside me and fingered his wolf-skin cloak, but I laid a restraining hand on his arm. "Gently," I hissed. "We are the strangers here." He relaxed with effort and I could see the strange woman smiling in amusement.

"Are you come far, then?" To my relief, she asked in our own tongue, her choice of words including us as distant kin. Disconcertingly, it was to Dyoan that she addressed her question.

He stared slack-jawed in amazement to hear that language from any lips but ours. I answered in his stead. "A long ways indeed since the beginning. From Dyelenol, but most recently from Ganasset."

She frowned, but it did not seem only in confusion. "Dyelenol?"

"Near Karskar in the north. Too far from lands where our people have settled, as it turned out. We are searching for a friendlier home."

She seemed to consider this and then make a decision. "We will offer you guesting, of course. It may be that the council will offer you more." She left that thought hanging vaguely and snapped her fingers at the hounds. They shed their skins and stood—a young man and woman who might have been twins, grinning at us as if to apologize for their earlier growls. She introduced the two of them and then sent them running back to the village to announce us.

So it was that they all turned out to welcome us—or almost all, as we learned. There were nearly fifty in the village, a circle of thatched huts set in a broad clearing. I could see Ale'en and Dyoan comparing it to their parents' fine stone house, but that house lay in ruins now far behind.

It took me a few minutes to put my finger on the oddness in these folk: the two hounds were the youngest who wore skins. There were no children at all with a furred or feathered cloak, and even a few adults went without. *They have no singer,* I thought. *No one to fashion new spell-songs. And so they are left only to pass down the old ones.* I'd heard of such clans before, of course, but it was a perilous way to survive. If someone died while cloaked, if no one learned the old song, there was one less skin for the clan. And an old song never had the power of one made for the wearer; it faded over the generations. Then I counted up the people I saw who wanted skins, and thought how long the making would be if they bound me to the task. It frightened me more than a little.

They led us into the long central hall, apologizing for the lack of merrymaking. "Grandmother is dying," one of the hounds explained, gesturing toward the hearth as they seated us and brought in food.

I looked where they pointed and saw a young brown-haired woman, and then looked again and saw that she held in her lap a bone-thin wildcat that she stroked slowly and gently. The woman who had come to greet us—Boesen, she was called—went over to her and said something sharply. The young woman looked up with tears in her eyes and answered, "It eases her pain. Why should you begrudge it?"

"Because we cannot afford to lose her skin," Boesen said, less sharply. "She knows that; don't encourage her."

The young woman gathered the cat in her arms as gently as possible and laid her on a pallet by the fire. "Gran, Gran," I heard her say, then something too soft to be understood. The skin fell away and a withered old woman lay on it, her gasping breath a pain to hear.

Boesen laid a hand on the younger woman's shoulder. "Ashóli, come to dinner. There is nothing you can do here."

"There *is* something I can do," she answered, taking the old woman's hand and settling herself by the bedside.

The other woman shrugged and turned away.

I felt as if I had been intruding, though no one else seemed to mark the exchange. Dyoan and Ale'en had been ensconced in the place for honored guests—much to their astonished delight—while I was seated down along one end with the younger folk. Given what I had seen, I guessed the reason.

They fed us on roasted pork and porridge and passed bowls of fresh milk around the table. And then when the meal was done, and the bowls were being filled with beer instead, the children and those who wore no skins drew back against the walls and Boesen began the chant that opened council.

They asked Dyoan our names—since it would have been rude to inquire before feeding us—and he gave them, the full and formal names with clan and parentage attached. But when he would have given me the honorific of a singer, I interrupted him with something inconsequential about my homeland, and made sure to catch his eye and shake my head in warning.

Boesen frowned in my direction. "You are a stranger and so we forgive your ignorance, but children may only speak in council when asked."

It was hard not to laugh, seeing Ale'en sitting there stiff with eight-year-old dignity in their midst. But she meant the other sense of "children," those who did not yet wear skins. In a clan where those were limited, it would be an important mark of adulthood. I looked over at the woman called Ashóli and wondered why she wore none when several younger than her sat in council.

The talk went much as I could have predicted: where did we come from; where were we going; did we know of kinfolk in the area? It seemed they were isolated here and were as eager as we to learn of others of our kind. Dyoan was handling the questions as well as I would have, so I set myself to studying the people instead, until my attention was jerked back by my own name.

"You are not Laaki's kin, you say, but surely you could serve as such for her. Is she married or betrothed?"

Dyoan looked wildly in my direction for help, but I shrugged so he answered simply, "No."

"Ah," Boesen said, nodding. "Then perhaps we can make a three-fold bargain with you. Your friend lacks a skin. We may soon have a skin available." She made a sign to ward off evil, but it was clear it was an empty gesture. "And my son, Goalnen, would like to take a bride. As the first bargain, perhaps Laaki would take a skin as a bride-price?"

Dyoan had no chance to respond, for Ashóli had risen from the old woman's bedside and shrieked, "No!"

"Ashóli, be still!" Boesen snapped.

"No! You can't! She said it should come to me."

"'Should' is not 'will'. We have to think of what's best for the family."

"And Goalnen is family, but I am not!" I could see Ashóli was shaking with rage, but she said no further word and dashed out the door.

Boesen made a calming gesture. "We needn't decide now. Tomorrow will be soon enough to begin the bargaining." Then she closed the council and we were shown places to sleep: the boys in the young men's lodgings and I alone in the guesthouse.

Dyoan slipped out to see me before going to sleep. I was expecting him. He looked around outside to make sure no one was in earshot then asked me quietly but heatedly, "Why did you let them treat you like that? You're a *byal-dónen*, a song-maker. They have no right to call you a child!"

"Peace!" I said. "We're guests here and you know only your own family's ways. I've seen this before: counting only skin-wearers as fully adult."

"But you had a skin, and you'll have one again." I could see a flicker of guilt cross his features, even in the dim light of the hut, as he recalled his own foolish part in the loss of my owl-skin.

"And if they know I am a skin-singer..." I wondered how much to tell him of the geas laid on my kind. "When your father left you and Ale'en in my care, it was not only kindness that made me care for you—though kindness would have been enough, I swear to you. Those that know the way of it can bind a song-maker to her task. He knew it, and when he knew there was no time for any other bargain, he bound me to make songs for you. I could not have left you until the task was done. Oh, I don't blame him for it," I said hastily, seeing the expression on Dyoan's face. "He was being hunted and needed to know you would be cared for. And if he had lived, he would have bargained properly for the work. But there it is. I could be many years making songs for these folk if they know. And I'm not so sure yet that I would be happy settling here."

"I didn't know..." Dyoan began.

"But now you do, and you will hold your tongue."

He nodded and slipped back to his own quarters.

On the next day, we were to talk further of the three-fold bargain. It was a ritual of our people, to bind us together with a triple exchange. A marriage offer would be a tricky thing to refuse, but if we insisted on an exchange they would not countenance, we could force *them* to withdraw the negotiations.

But that morning Goalnen began courting me and I began to think of other things than escape. He was only a little older than me, and not at all bad to look upon. And though I put little stock in his flowery words, I could see he was intelligent and generous and knew how to laugh. So I told Dyoan to stall them with details while I considered what answer I wanted to give.

And then, in the midst of that bright day, the old woman died and all else was put aside to mourn her. There was little to prepare; they had been ready for her death most of the spring. They took turns singing her soul on its journey, and Ashóli stubbornly insisted on watching through the night along with her uncles and aunt, although she had no true right to keep vigil. The next day, they buried the old woman with her belongings except, of course, for the cat-skin. Boesen had taken it from her body before it was cold, lest it bind her soul to the world, and perhaps to lay claim to its disposal.

The boys and I did honor at her graveside, though we had not known her. But when I looked up across the fresh earth and met Ashóli's stare I knew there would be trouble. It was hard not to sympathize with her, for I had gathered her story from whispered gossip. She had been her grandmother's favorite and yet, because her mother had been a second wife and clanless, no one else would take her part. Ashóli had been passed over for skins several times. This was likely her last chance. Even now there was no guarantee it would go to her if I refused Goalnen. If I accepted him, the skin would be mine, and there was nothing to say I had to keep it for myself. But Ashóli could not know that I had no need of another's skin.

And so I lay awake that night, alone in the guesthouse and listened for noises in the dark. She came, finally, as the sky was just beginning to brighten, the time when most people sleep the deepest. I heard a rustling by the door too loud and deliberate for a mouse. I tried to breathe slowly and evenly as I heard her cross the floor.

She stood for a long time, accustoming her eyes to the dimness. Then she bent over me and raised one hand with the glint of a knife. My hand shot up and grabbed her wrist, bending it sharply until her fingers loosened. I heard her gasp in surprise and fear but she did not cry out. I pushed the knife aside and pulled myself up and her down so we sat facing.

"You foolish girl," I whispered. "A little patience could have got what you wanted, and more. I don't need another's skin."

Ashóli stared in confusion, then her eyes widened. "*Byal-dónen*?"

I nodded, wrapping myself in what I hoped was intimidating dignity.

"Then why..." she began. I saw hope chase the questions from her eyes and they grew wild with wanting. "Take me away with you. Make a skin for me—I'll do whatever you ask. I'll be your servant; I'll do anything. Only don't leave me here to see another wear my skin."

"Your skin?" I was surprised by her possessiveness. "Did the old woman name it yours, then?" She might have learned the skin's song by listening, but knowing a song was not ownership.

She dropped her eyes but dared not lie to me. "No. Boesen forbade it, and Gran didn't have the strength to oppose her. But I could not bear to see it go to another after I had..." Her voice trailed off and she seemed frightened at what she had begun to say.

I made a guess and finished for her. "After you had worn it yourself."

She nodded miserably.

"And what good would killing me have done?" I asked. "Did you think no one would figure it out with a guest slain under their own roof?"

She stared at me in dawning horror. *Guest-slayer*: the very word was unthinkable. The depth of her desperation showed in her failure to admit, even to herself, what she had planned.

"How did you learn the skin-song," I asked curiously. "Did she teach you or did you overhear."

"I didn't...I didn't mean to. It wasn't like that," she stammered. "It was one night when Gran was asleep. I only put the skin-cloak around me—to see how it would feel. I didn't mean any harm. I think I just *wanted* too much. And then...then I changed."

My astonishment must have shown on my face because she flinched back, thinking my reaction was to her transgression.

"But don't you see? I can't stay, not if they give Gran's cat-skin to someone else."

My mind was racing. Clearly she had no idea what it meant—that she had worn another's skin, without a changing-song, by will alone. They had the answer to their problems at hand and no one here had the wit or knowledge to see it.

A plan formed in my mind. I picked the knife up and put it back in her fingers, heedless of her confusion. Then I dragged her by the wrist out into the growing dawn. A few early risers stared at us curiously. I took a deep breath and began chanting the call for the three-fold bargain.

"*Geol-dón, geol-dón anaol,*
Geol-dón, geol-dón byenol,
Geol-dón alyen ambol."

As I began it a second time, people were boiling out of the buildings like angry ants. Boesen broke through the clustering throng, took in the frightened Ashóli, still holding her knife, and demanded, "What does this mean?" She tried to ignore me and searched out Dyoan in the crowd. "What is this disturbance?"

He stepped up beside me. "Laaki has a tongue of her own. Ask her. She called for the bargaining."

"Does she speak in your name, then?" Boesen asked.

"If you like," he said with a shrug. He went back to stand by Ale'en and waited with eager curiosity.

When Boesen turned her attention to me, I sat on the ground before her—as one does for bargain-making—and pulled Ashóli down to sit beside me.

"I have a set of bargains to propose," I began, following the traditional words. "For each, you will tell me whether you think it a fair bargain or not."

I could tell she was angry, but now she was caught in the ceremony and would have to see it through. She sat before us and the rest of the village gathered round.

"This one," I said, pointing to Ashóli, "has broken your hospitality."

Ashóli shot me a terrified, pleading look as the crowd began to mutter.

"You owe me a price for the attack made against me while I was under your protection."

"She will die," Boesen said flatly.

I held up my hand in ritual denial. "I do not accept the bargain. It is your family that must pay the price."

Boesen pressed her lips together grimly. "She is a miserable creature, but she is one of our clan."

"Is she?" I asked sharply. "And if she is of your clan, why was she denied the skin that should have been hers? Was that not a rejection of her as much as if you had closed your doors to her? I say she has no family and cannot pay your price for you."

It was a subtle argument, and I would have been hard pressed to convince a law-singer with it. But there was guilt here over how they had treated Ashóli, and I blew that from embers into a flame.

"Will you suggest a bargain, then?" Boesen asked warily.

I pretended to consider for a minute. "As the price of the crime against me, I will take your vengeance." There was confused talk all around me but Boesen only waited patiently for the explanation. She saw the game, though not how the pieces moved. "Give me your right to revenge against Ashóli as the price of your failure to protect me. Though she did not break her own hospitality, she broke yours, and owes you a price for that. Give me her debt in exchange for your own."

Boesen gave Ashóli a look that suggested she was not entirely unhappy to let it go. "I accept this bargain," she said.

Then I turned to Ashóli herself. "Now your debt is to me. I will bargain for it. For the price you owe, I will take three years of your life in service."

I could see the relief sweep over her, though she did not yet understand the whole of it. "It is a fair bargain," she answered. It was much what she had offered earlier when she begged to leave with me.

Boesen cut in hurriedly. "For the third bargain, will you consider the one we spoke of before? The skin as your bride-price?"

I looked up at Goalnen and smiled faintly to try to soften my answer as I made the sign of refusal again. "I do not accept the bargain. I find I have no wish to be a bought wife. But bring the skin and I will offer for it. You will tell me if the bargain is fair."

Boesen frowned, but she signaled to her son. Goalnen went and got it and laid it on the ground between the three of us. As he passed, I could see that my choice had disappointed him. I reached out and touched the soft spotted fur of the cloak. It took all Ashóli's will not to do the same.

"Here is my bargain," I said. "Give me the cat-skin and in three years I will trade you a song-maker for it."

There was a stunned silence from the crowd. Boesen finally found her tongue to speak. "It is a handsome bargain, as you well know. There would be no fame for me in refusing. You are a *byal-dónen*?"

I shrugged. "Perhaps I am, perhaps I'm not. It will be Ashóli I trade to you for it. She has the talent, and in three years she will have the skill as well."

Boesen looked the girl over with a newly measuring eye. Ashóli in turn was gaping at me in surprise. But understanding crept over her, and she turned to face her aunt with a quiet confidence born of her new status.

I knew then that my meddling would bear sweet fruit, not bitter. There was no hatred between them, only an uneasy reassessment of their positions.

Boesen nodded, answering the unspoken question. "The bargain is well-made. *Gyel-dón a-don.* And I think we have all received more than we have given."

"The best sort of bargain," I agreed. "*Gyel-don a-dón.*"

I took up the skin-cloak and draped it over Ashóli's shoulders as she rose. I could see Goalnen watching approvingly from the edge of the crowd. *And perhaps,* I thought, *when three years are done, I will return them two skin-singers after all.*

By the Skin of Her Teeth

"**H**ave I told you of how I learned I was to be a skin-singer?"

I saw the corners of Ashóli's mouth twitch, and I could almost hear her thinking, *Ah, no! Not more old stories!* But she spread her cat-skin cloak on the ground beside the fire and sat, listening, as the flames threw sparks up into the growing twilight. I saw her thoughts wandering as I recounted the tale. For three years she had eagerly drunk in my teaching; now she was growing restless.

When she suddenly came alert, I wondered what I had said to recapture her attention. Then I, too, heard what she had cocked her head to listen for. Somewhere up the mountainside, someone was racing a horse through the near-darkness, a horse that was spent and staggering.

We had set our small shelter in a clearing on the road running up toward the pass. It was near enough to Ashóli's village that they could bring us food and news easily, but far enough that we would not be constantly interrupted. (Far enough that when her cousin Goalnen came courting me it was a pleasant break and not a constant nuisance.) Several times in each year, traders would come across and down, bringing tools and fine cloth and other things it was not worth our trouble to make ourselves. And more often than that, some of Ashóli's people would travel up and over taking furs and carvings and fine needlework and other things they had made to barter.

But this was no trader with slow, surefooted mules. I wondered that the rider had made it along the steep mountain track at that pace without a mortal fall. The hoofbeats came closer and more erratically, and Ashóli and I rose as one and cast our skin-cloaks about our shoulders, ready for what might befall.

She stumbled into the circle of firelight and fell, more than dismounted, from the lathered gray mare beneath her. I was surprised at how young she was—younger than Ashóli, perhaps. She had a different look than the others that traveled that same path, smaller and darker. She looked wildly from the one of us to the other and cried something in a language that was strange to me. Seeing our incomprehension, she tried again in the language that the traders use.

"Please, you must help me! He's coming... He will kill me. I didn't do it. It wasn't my fault, but he won't believe me."

I don't know what I would have tried to ask first, but at that moment the mare gave a sighing grunt and fell heavily to the ground. The woman echoed her cry and ran to take the horse's head in her lap as the deep brown eyes began to glaze over in death. She began a high keening, in harsh, tearing sobs. I stood stupidly, at a loss for what to do, but Ashóli crouched beside her to stroke the mare's head and softly croon the death-song, the one we sing to release those whose skins we take. I don't know whether she had any thought at the time of cloak-making, I think it was simply the only way she knew to share the woman's sorrow at the death. Later...well, but that was later.

By the time Ashóli finished her song, the woman had finished her weeping and, haltingly, began her tale with the horse.

"I raised her from a foal," she said softly, as if talking to herself. "She was always my darling, my swift one, my Sunna. I took her as part of my dowry when they wed me to Gorliv. And whatever happened after that, I could be a girl again on her back—a maiden racing over the hills of home. I never wanted to marry a stranger, but it was a good alliance, and I did what my kin expected of me. I longed to have a child—though it terrified me—and Gorliv wanted sons. But then the boy died, before he was even named. It happens sometimes," she pleaded, looking up at us as if we were accusers. "Sometimes a babe is sickly and it just dies. There's no need for blame. But he said I had witched it, to strike at him. And they believed him. I had no one to speak for me, so I ran."

She looked back up the trail as if expecting pursuit to follow at any moment and her terror was so close that I, too, listened for following hoofbeats. "He won't give up. He will track me down and kill me. He swore it."

I spoke for the first time since she had arrived. "And so you will lead him here and make trouble for us."

Ashóli leapt up and faced me angrily. "Laaki! How can you say such a thing? She has come to us a stranger; we owe her guest-right."

I answered in the Kaltaoven tongue so that the woman would not understand. "Can't you see? Her husband will come here hunting witches, and he will find them. She isn't one of us. The peddlers who come here—they know how to keep a tongue behind the teeth if they want to deal with us. But I have seen what happens when strangers find us out. Do you want your kinfolk killed or driven off to live as beasts? I have *seen* it."

Ashóli was frightened for a moment, not knowing whether I spoke of past memories or fore-seeing. "And what if he doesn't come?" she protested. "What if she lost him on the trail? You can't be sure she's brought danger down on us."

"He'd be a fool if he's on that track tonight," I said. "But I mean to see for myself."

I strode up the trail, out of the firelight and out of sight, before pulling my owl-feathers closely around me. I whispered the skin-song that drew their essence into me. *Él-taov alyev, mél-daegh alyev, Time to wear the feathers, time to fly the night.* And then I spread my wings and soared silently over the tree-covered slopes and up to where the mountain track rose along the rocky heights, listening with the owl's ears. Nothing stirred there that did not belong. If he was coming, it was not tonight.

When I flew back home, there was no sign of the stranger-woman in the yard around the dying fire, but I shed my feathers out of sight to be safe. Ashóli met me in the door to our hut with a finger on her lips.

"I've sung her to sleep. Morning will be soon enough to sort things out."

"And send her on her way," I said sharply. "What more have you learned?"

She gave me a troubled glance. "Her name is Eysla. I told her she could stay as long as she needed to."

"What?" I was startled by how angry I felt.

"Laaki, what's wrong with you? She needs help."

"Help is for our kind, for Kaltaoven." I spoke to her as if she were a child, and perhaps that was a mistake. "We don't owe anything to strangers."

"I was a stranger to you," she answered quietly. "I wasn't your kin; you didn't owe me anything. But when my own family would have cast me out, you took my part. Why?"

I was too angry to answer. It wasn't the same at all and I thought she was baiting me. I cast my feathers around me again and went off to hunt the night.

When I returned in the morning, tired but purged of my anger, I found Ashóli and the stranger flaying the mare's carcass. "When you've finished," I said to Ashóli, "go fetch some help from the village to finish the butchering. No need for waste."

She shook her head.

The stranger looked at her curiously. "I don't mind. It's only meat now, the rest of her is in my heart."

"No," Ashóli said. "It's forbidden to us."

"Because she died and was not properly killed? But surely you have dogs to feed..."

"No, because—"

"Do you plan to make a skin-cloak, then?" I interrupted, shifting back into our own tongue. "From a beast of burden?" It was the only reason I could think of to declare the flesh taboo.

Ashóli shrugged and quoted an old proverb. "'Who can know what skin will fit?' She was a noble beast, and it will be a new test for me."

The stranger was watching us with no comprehension, waiting to be told—or not—as we saw fit. Her bland complacency irritated me anew. I wondered that she'd had the courage to run at all. When she saw me frowning at her, she stood and came to kneel before me, which did nothing to change my mood.

"Get up, stranger," I said roughly.

"She has a name," Ashóli protested.

I searched my memory. "Get up, Eysla."

She rose to her feet. "Ashóli tells me that I must have your permission to stay here. I will be no burden, I promise you. I can cook and sew and fetch water, and run errands to the village for you. Ashóli tells me that you are often too busy with her training."

"'Ashóli tells me,'" I mimicked. "What else does Ashóli tell you?"

Eysla stared at me blankly.

I turned to Ashóli. "Well? What else?" I changed to the Kaltaoven tongue again. "Have you told her what we are? Have you told her what she will see down in the village?"

"No, Laaki, I swear! I've been careful."

I turned back to Eysla. "This is as much Ashóli's home as it is mine. If she calls you a guest, that is her choice, but do not expect me to make you welcome. Now I am tired and will thank you to leave me in peace for a while."

When I woke late in the afternoon, I found the two of them laughing softly over some task as if they had been sisters. Of a sudden, I understood Ashóli's rebellion better. She had always been the outcast—lowest and forgotten by her clan—before I saw that she could be a skin-singer. Now here was the first person she had ever known who not only treated her as an equal, but looked up to her. Understanding that did not lessen the danger.

They had managed to dispose of the horse's carcass, piece by piece, far enough that the scavengers would not bother us. Ashóli had cut the skin into a rough cloak-shape and pegged it out to dry. I saw Eysla glance at it curiously from time to time, but I didn't ask what explanation Ashóli had given her.

It was easier than I thought to get used to Eysla's presence. She was quiet and never underfoot. We were fed better cooking in the next three days than we had been in the three years before. And when it was time for Ashóli's lessons and I made a pretense of sending Eysla to the creek for water, she took the jug and asked bluntly when she should return. But I knew it could never last.

One day just past dawn, as we sat eating our morning meal, there came a skittering of paws running up the path toward us and a lean, brindled hound burst into our yard. Before I could move to stop him, Ashóli's young cousin stood and shed his hound-skin before us.

Eysla screamed and jumped to her feet. The boy gaped in dismay, realizing his mistake. Ashóli went for the one and I the other. I couldn't hear what Ashóli was saying, but I scolded the boy so sharply I could almost see his ears droop and the tail creep between his legs. And after all that, his news was of little enough moment to make him so careless.

When I had sent him scampering back home, I turned anxiously to see what had happened with Eysla. I expected her to have run, to have gone mad with fear. Oh, she was frightened, that was clear enough. But Ashóli had drawn her away and was speaking softly and rapidly in her ear. I saw Eysla reach out to touch the spotted fur of Ashóli's cloak, then snatch her hand back as if burned. I let them be—though I doubted how much good mere words would do—and set about the day's chores. It was a long time before the other two joined me again.

There was a long, heavy silence between us as we worked, but after a time Eysla said, "I have wondered what it would be like."

I glanced at her questioningly.

"I used to dream of *being* Sunna sometimes, of running four-footed over the hills and being free of what everyone demanded of me."

I gave a short barking laugh. "Is that all the freedom you can dream of? To be bound with saddle and bridle and bear some man upon your back? That seems to me little different from the life you led."

She looked away then, but Ashóli was staring at her with that far-off look in her eyes. If I had known what she was thinking, I would have sent Eysla packing at once, no matter what the danger.

But I didn't suspect what Ashóli had in mind until several days later. I had gone down to the village on some excuse, but mostly because it had been too long since I had seen Goalnen. There was an understanding between us, but it didn't pay to depend on understandings. When I returned the next afternoon, the mare-skin was gone from its place and neither Ashóli nor Eysla were to be found. I was filled with dread then, hoping that I was wrong.

I ran to the meadow where we had been doing Ashóli's lessons and found her sitting on a stone, watching a gray mare running in the clearing below.

"What have you done?" I demanded. "She isn't Kaltaoven! You will drive her mad trapping her in a skin like that." And then, at the far end of the meadow, I saw the horse shift to a woman, who waved back at us. It was too far to hear the words, but I saw her pull the skin-cloak tighter about her and turn again to horse. "You made a song for her," I said in horror.

Ashóli had turned to me, her eyes shining with excitement. "But don't you see? It's the song that has the power, not the singer, or even the tongue it's in. *Anyone* can wear a skin."

I took her by the shoulders and shook her like a naughty child. "Did you think this was something new? Did you think no one else had ever tried such a thing before? Of course outsiders can learn our songs; I've seen it before. And it always means death and disaster for us. They have no sense, no traditions, no clan. They go crazy with it, and we get blamed. What were you thinking of?"

"I was thinking that she wanted it," Ashóli answered, subdued but still stubborn. "She begged for it—to know what it was like. And I wanted to see if I could do it. She can learn what she needs."

"From whom?" I asked. "Your clan will never take her in. And her own people would call her a sorceress, as they would call us."

"She can learn from me," she said defiantly.

I let go of her shoulders and tried one more time. "And what of your duty to your clan? What of the songs you owe them?"

"Do I?" she asked. "That was *your* bargain—to give them a skin-singer. Mine was to give you the last three years. I've given them nine skin-songs in the past year—plus the two still unclaimed—so any debt is paid. You will marry Goalnen and stay; what need do they have of me?"

In her voice, I could hear a decision made long since that had nothing to do with Eysla. "So what will you do?" I asked.

Her eyes took on their far-away look. "I want to travel—like you have. I want to *see* things, to dream things."

It struck me to the heart. "Child, do you think that I've been wandering by my own choice? Every home I have ever had was destroyed by the greed and fear of outsiders. You should not envy me." It was no use; I could see that.

Hooves thudded behind us, then changed to a tentative footstep. "Ashóli...?

I turned on Eysla and said harshly, "You're a fool."

She flinched from me, but no longer in fear. Wearing the skin-cloak had made that change in her.

"Perhaps you knew no better," I said more mildly, "but Ashóli should have."

She slipped the mare-skin from her shoulders and clutched it tightly to her breast. "You will not take Sunna away from me. I won't lose her again." She looked to Ashóli for support.

I sighed. It was too late for going back. We would have to play the game out to its end.

It had been long enough that I had begun to think there would be no pursuit. But the next morning, a trick of the cool, still air brought the faint baying of hounds, drifting down the mountainside. I could not fly out to see during the daylight, so Ashóli took the cloak of raven feathers that had not yet gone to a wearer from where it hung by the also-unclaimed fox-cloak. There was hardly a need for her sharp eyes to confirm what we had heard. Three riders—with twice as many dogs—were picking their way down from the pass. There was nothing else they could be hunting. I sent Ashóli flying down to warn the village. When she had gone, I made my way back to our camp, hardening myself for what must be done.

Eysla was kneeling beside the outdoor hearth, kneading dough in a trough. I don't know why it bothered me to see her doing such homely things, as if she thought she could make everything right by being a better, more dutiful wife for someone.

"They have come hunting you," I said with no attempt to soften the news. "They came through the pass this morning with dogs and horses. I've sent Ashóli down to warn her kin."

She stared at me dumbly for a moment, then rocked back on her heels and stood, brushing the flour from her hands.

I was angry at her seeming unconcern. "You brought this down on us—on Ashóli. If they find us out; we cannot let them leave. Yet if they do not return more will come, and more, and in the end, we will be driven from our homes just the same."

She winced at that. Saying nothing, she disappeared into the hut. I started after her, but she reappeared at once, clasping the gray mare's skin about her shoulders.

"What are you doing?" I demanded, though I could guess easily enough.

"What I always do," she answered with a strange smile on her lips. "What you expect me to do; always what others expect me to do."

"And how long do you think you can keep running?" I asked.

She shook her head. "You don't understand: not what you fear, but what you expect. I shouldn't have to run very long." She closed her eyes and drew the skin around her tightly as she chanted the song Ashóli had made for her. It made me sick to hear a skin-song in a foreign tongue. It was wrong, desperately wrong. Hooves thudded on the hardened earth of our yard as she found her feet and ran.

Even as I heard her hoofbeats fading over the crest of the ridge, the faint baying of the hounds came drifting nearer. They were making no secret of their presence, hoping, no doubt, to flush her out. And so she would satisfy them. It was far from the best solution. If they spread tales of skin-changers in this valley... But there was no reason they should know there were others here at all. They had come chasing a witch and now they would find her.

Ashóli returned with a fluttering of wings and had to pause to catch her breath before making her report. "They will be ready if the hunt comes down to the village. Where is Eysla?"

She looked around and her eyes fell on the kneading trough by the fire, with the dough crusting over in the heat, and then she saw the hoof tracks leading out of the yard. "Where is she?" she repeated. "What have you done?"

"I've done nothing," I said. "She chose her own course."

Ashóli faced me, her face white with rage and sorrow. "How could she choose when you offered her nothing else? You drove her back to him because you haven't the courage to find another way."

"It isn't a matter of courage," I answered hotly, "but of wisdom. I can't make the whole world right, and if I must choose, I'll choose to protect my clan."

"*My* clan is large enough to include her, just as yours was once large enough to include me." She took on the raven-skin again, though she looked too exhausted to fly much further, and set off in the direction of the sounds of the hunt.

What could I do? I followed her. Since my feathers were useless in daylight and I would not take Ashóli's cat-skin without permission, I chose the waiting fox-cloak—good for swift running and sharp ears and nose. But she was flying over the broken ridges and deep gullies of the mountainside, and I must take the longer ways.

It seemed like hours that I ran through brush and bramble, but finally the scent of blood drew me away from the sounds of the hunt and down into a sheltered hollow. Eysla hid there with her back against a stone, a bloody arrow at her side and her thigh wrapped with what had once been Ashóli's tunic.

"Where is she?" I demanded.

Her eyes fluttered open and she gritted her teeth as she turned toward me. "I tried to stop her," she said tightly. "They would have found me soon enough and it would have been over. I showed myself to them, then changed and taunted Gorliv, then changed again and ran. I might have led them back over the pass before they ran me down but for *that*." She gestured toward the feathered shaft. "I tried to stop her, but she would not hear. And when she had bound my leg, she put on the mare's skin and took the feathers into her and led them on past."

I could hear the sounds of the hunt far off in the distance—too far for fox-legs to catch up with now. Eysla struggled to her feet and reached to me for support. I helped her climb up out of the hollow and onto the ridge where we could see.

The hunt had gone up beyond the trees along the rocky paths leading toward the pass. The gray horse scudded along the road like a patch of fog. They must have wondered at her renewed speed; surely they had seen the blood. Behind her ran the dogs, and behind them, the three horsemen. They climbed along the scree, the mare in wild unconcern, the hunters more slowly, following a track traced across the mountainside that we could barely see. The path disappeared behind a bend just ahead of where the gray horse ran, and where it turned, the mountainside fell steeply, nearly straight down, for a very long way.

I held my breath as she neared the bend, guessing what would come next. The mare never slackened her pace, and where the track turned back out of sight, she gathered her legs under her and leapt out into the void.

Beside me, Eysla screamed. I grabbed at her and forced her gaze back toward the distant mountainside. "Look! There!"

The gray shape had fallen so slowly, as if in a dream. And now it seemed to collapse in on itself and a black shadow slipped from under it just before it hit the rocks below. Eysla took a deep, ragged breath. "How could she...?"

"She still had the raven-skin, you said. But even so, I doubt I would have dared a change like that." I looked back to the trackway far above. The riders had dismounted and were peering over the edge. Too long a fall to survive; too deep a chasm to be worth climbing down to check. Ashóli knew these tracks like the palm of her hand. I had no doubt she had planned that leap carefully and marked the place to retrieve the horse-cloak later.

After a while, the hunters moved on, further up the trail toward the pass and home. And Eysla and I headed home as well, more slowly and with much pain for her. Finally I made her sit and cast the fox-skin around her shoulders. "If you will permit it," I said, "I will be able to carry you the rest of the way." I wouldn't trap myself in the same body with her, but I could lighten the burden.

She was startled, and looked up at me suspiciously. "I thought you didn't approve of outsiders wearing skins."

I sighed. "I will not pretend to be happy about it, but perhaps the lines are not so clearly drawn. If Ashóli has claimed you as chosen-kin, I will not deny you." It seemed that Ashóli had begun teaching her the Kaltaoven tongue, for she started in surprise when I used the in-clan inflection as I whispered, "*Kael-taov adye.* Wear thy skin!"

I gathered the little lame fox up in my arms and headed home, to where Ashóli would be waiting.

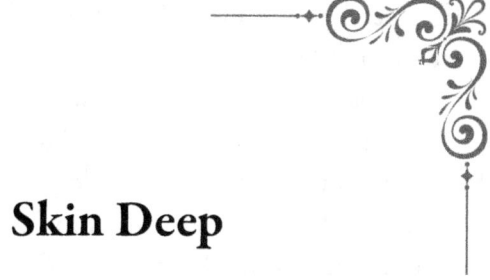

Skin Deep

When I finished my apprenticeship as a skin-singer and left my home to see more of the world, my teacher, Laaki, made me promise to keep all that I saw and did in memory, to tell her when I returned. I did not think, at that time, that it was certain I *would* return. And I do not think, now, that I will tell all of my stories. But still, I have kept them all remembered.

Eysla and I had left the last village two days behind and traveled up from the green farmlands in the river valley into the scrubby hills. From here, there was too much chance of encountering someone who knew Gorliv, Eysla's husband. Gorliv believed his errant wife to be dead and it was best he continued to think so.

As the road leveled out on the high, rolling plains, Eysla moved into an easy trot beneath me, and then to a canter. She liked to run; I was coming to love it as well. We Kaltaoven rarely kept horses. Why spend your stores to feed a dumb beast when your own skin-shape can carry you as swiftly? But Eysla had invited me to ride and I had learned slowly, hampered by the lack of a saddle and the other things one would have used with a beast-horse. Even if we'd had them, that would have presumed too far.

The road—more of a track at this point—stretched out through the high grass and scattered brush pointing toward the distant mountains. We had seen deer in the distance and geese flying overhead, and I was only momentarily startled when a partridge burst from the grass nearly at our feet. But Eysla jumped sideways from the bird's flight and hit the ground racing as if for her life. I clamped my legs about her and grabbed for her neck, shouting her name. Her ears were flattened back and did not even flick in acknowledgment. I shouted again. I could feel myself slipping and watched the ground speeding past in a blur. In the moment I fell, I sang my cat-skin about me, hoping to land lightly as I hit the bushes. A hidden rock stopped my roll with a crunch of pain and the taste of copper. In the clarity of the moment, I could hear Eysla's hoofbeats fading in the distance.

I must have fainted, for the next thing I knew was Eysla's voice crying, "Ashóli, Ashóli!" over and over again, and the feel of her hand stroking my fur. I blinked and saw her crouching over me with tears in her eyes. But there seemed no damage done beyond a bitten tongue. I tested my body in cat-form first, then shed my skin and let her help me to my feet.

"What happened?" I asked, trying to keep the accusation from my voice.

She looked down at the ground. "I was going to ask you that. I was so far gone from my mind... The first thing I knew was when you were not on my back."

I took her by the shoulder and forced her to face me. "What do you mean 'gone from my mind'?"

She fingered the gray horse skin that hung as a cloak about her shoulders—the one that had been a living mare the night she had fled, terrified, into Laaki's firelight and my life. "It's what I've told you: when I become Sunna, sometimes my mind flies away. I know I shouldn't," she protested hurriedly. "But it's so good just to *be* her, with no thoughts and cares beyond what a horse would think."

I sighed deeply. This was what Laaki had warned me. When I made a skin-song for an outsider—for someone who had not been born Kaltaoven—there were dangers that I could never have imagined. To hear her speak so casually of something so monstrous!

"Eysla," I said, as gently and patiently as I could. "You don't 'become' Sunna. Your mare is dead. When you wear her skin, you are never anything but yourself. The skin has body-memories, so that you need not learn to walk and run anew, but that is all. If you abandon your humanity in *this* body—" I touched her cheek to draw her eyes to mine. "—people call it madness. It is no less madness if you are wearing a skin. Do you find my company so tiresome that you need that escape?"

"Ashóli, no!" she cried instantly. "I'm sorry. But I think you are wrong. Sunna is in there with me; I can feel her."

I let it pass. She was so quickly contrite, but so strange in her thinking. Perhaps it was only that "Sunna" was the name she gave to the body-memory. Perhaps she needed to wear other skins to understand the difference. I looked around for our bags. "Where have you left our things?"

She, too, looked around and then laughed. "I left them back where I turned around. When I found you had fallen, I changed—I wasn't thinking. And then when I put my skin on again, I couldn't take the baggage inside my skin. It seems so easy when you help!"

I smiled and forbore from pointing out that she managed it with her clothes nicely enough. Such a trouble it would be if we must be naked under our skins!

I found I was limping a little by the time we had collected our things, and Eysla insisted that we go no farther than the next creek to make camp for the day, even though there were several hours until dusk. She cut some willows from the bank to set up our little shelter and began fixing a meal for herself. I put on my fur and went to seek my own, in spite of the creeping stiffness. Eysla ate more cheaply in human form, but I could do better as a cat.

I came back well-satisfied but limping even more and stretched out beside the small fire she had built, without shedding my skin. Eysla reached over and ran her hand along my back. I half-closed my eyes and encouraged her with a purr. I wished she would touch me like that in human form. When I shed my skin, she pulled her hand away and blushed furiously. I felt it like a slap. "I am *myself*, whether I wear a skin or not! I'm not your pet cat." Then I turned away to another task, not trusting myself to say more.

Eysla began, "I'm sorry, I didn't mean..."

I cut her off short. "I know what you didn't mean." What hurt was that I wanted her to mean it.

There was a long, empty silence between us as we set things in order for the night. It was Eysla who broke it at last, on safer ground. "You should rest a few days, to make sure it's just bruises and nothing worse."

She was right, but I heard something else behind her words. "I thought we were nearly to your family's stead. You said another day..."

She nodded.

I saw where this was leading. "You can't mean we should rest there! Just ride in and out, you said—that's all you wanted. You can't mean to live in a horse's skin for three or four days while we tarry there."

"If I must. It will be better for you."

"And for you? Can you do that and not betray yourself? You are dead to them, remember. When I agreed to this, we said it would be quick, like a peddler passing through. Not to—"

Eysla cut me off. "The accident was my fault. Let me pay for it."

There was no answer to that. It wasn't her willingness I doubted, only her ability.

I would have missed the place, but for Eysla's certainty. Trees were scarce here in the high plains, but stone and turf were plentiful. So it was that the buildings of her family's holdings appeared as just a few more hills on first inspection. We had seen scattered herds of horses and sheep for some time, and sometimes a glimpse of those who tended them. Eysla assured me that word of our arrival would be known long before we came into the turf-walled yard. The place held not one family, in truth, but a vast and sprawling clan, much like my own village had. A great number of them turned out to greet us, emerging from the sunken houses like rabbits up from a warren.

"I have goods to trade," I told them in the tongue that Eysla and I had first shared. Now, what with me teaching her the Kaltaoven language, and with her teaching me her own, we ended up speaking between us in a soup that was neither one thing nor the other. But it was best that I keep to the traders' tongue here and avoid questions of how I had learned theirs.

I hoisted our bags down into the waiting hands—we could hardly carry them the usual way this time—and then slipped down from Eysla's back. I winced more than a little as I hit the ground. Eysla was staring around her with an intensity that I feared must seem strange in a horse. I put my hand on her nose to get her attention and whispered, "*Ni'adorna!* Not so human!" She snorted and tried to look less interested as I opened up the bundle with our trade goods and spread them out for inspection.

That part was no fiction; we had to make a living somehow in our travels. We had started out with a load of the jewelry and fine carvings and the other small things that my people made for trade. There was still some of that left, but in a vast mixture of other goods. The hardest part, I had learned, was guessing what things the next town or village would want, not simply what the current one had to offer.

If it had been our original plan, I would have pushed people to choose quickly, but instead I stood back to let them look. I thought of Eysla's descriptions to see if I could identify any of her brothers or cousins. For the most part, they were all slightly-built, like her, and dark in coloring. I would have known any of them for her kin, but beyond that I could not tell one from the other. And then a man came in at the gate on a small black horse with a handful of dogs winding around his heels. And both from Eysla's description and from the behavior of those around me I knew that this must be her oldest brother, the one who had been burdened early with the care of his clan.

He invited me to stay for dinner—that was only courtesy. So I broached the subject of my fall and my need to rest, offering to bargain for my keep. We negotiated for a while, until the demands of hospitality and economy were both satisfied. He signaled for two boys to take my things inside, and then for another to take my horse. I was hard put convincing him that Eysla would be fine out on the hills with the other horses, but at last he shrugged and gave in. Eysla had insisted—for the sake of appearances—on a rope halter at the least, but I slipped it off now and turned her head toward the gate with a pat on her shoulder to send her out.

Her brother, Toral, watched intently with a bemused smile, commenting, "Such a well-trained beast to have thrown you."

For all their rough appearance from the outside, the turf-houses were neat and elegant within. The meal was plain, but satisfying, and I was given a chamber to myself for the night. There was no window, though, and I regretted not being able to slip out and speak to Eysla before going to sleep.

I slept long and soundly. And with no outside light, I did not know it was morning when I woke. I only knew that there was a horse screaming in fear somewhere outside. Then I recognized it for Eysla's skin-voice. I tore open the door and ran for the yard, scattering breakfasting children in my wake. Toral and several other men were there, clinging to ropes holding a gray mare who reared and plunged and cried out for help.

"Stop it!" I shouted, pulling away first one than another. Eysla broke free and spun away, trailing ropes from her neck. I could see no sign of the woman in her crazed eyes. I didn't dare call her by name, but I shouted in the Kaltaoven tongue, "Sister, wake up! I'm here!" She turned again with more sense in her eyes, her ribs heaving. I pushed through the men to her side, tearing the ropes from her neck angrily, and shouting at them, "Is this your hospitality? Is this how you behave to a guest?"

Toral came over and helped pull the last one free. "I meant no harm in bringing her in. She didn't used to go crazy at the touch of a rope."

It took a moment for his words to sink in. I tried to bluff it out. "What do you mean?"

"I know this horse. I trained her with my own hands and gave her to my sister on her wedding day. Odd that she returns here in a stranger's hands. How did you come by her?"

I groped for a plausible answer, but he didn't seem to notice.

He continued, "If I'd known Gorliv planned to sell her, I would have told him to name his price when he was here." He turned to me as if only just remembering my presence. "My sister died—so young! Her husband could not keep from weeping when he told me of it. I had no heart to reclaim her dowry from him, but this part I would have asked for if I'd known."

"How did she die?" I ventured, curious to know what story the falsely-mourning Gorliv had told.

"In childbirth, she and the babe both. She—"

I felt Eysla move under my hand, but had not even time to cry "No!" before she slipped from her horse's skin, shouting hotly, "That's a lie!"

Toral turned white. From across the yard I heard someone scream. I despaired of a way to turn this right again.

"That's a lie," Eysla repeated. "It was only the babe who died, but Gorliv said I witched it. He hunted me from his home and would not let me be until he had killed me."

I thought for a moment that Toral would kneel before her; he somehow gave that impression even though he stood. "Spirit of my sister," he whispered, "why do you tell me this? Have you come to demand vengeance for your death?"

Eysla was taken aback. And then she laughed, breaking the spell. "Toral, I'm not a ghost! He didn't kill me, he only thought he did. It's me." She reached her hand toward him but he jerked away. Her voice wavered. "Toral, it's me."

He shook his head. "You came to me as a gray horse. Death comes that way. Either tell me what you want or leave my family in peace. Please, if there is anything of Eysla in you, leave us in peace."

"I wanted to see everyone again," she answered softly. "I wanted to know you were well."

And then, cutting across those words of fear and pain, came a cry of pure joy and a small body hurtling across the yard. Toral tried to stop her, but the girl threw herself into Eysla's arms crowing, "Eysha! Eysha!"

Eysla held her tightly and looked past to Toral, saying, "You see? I'm not a ghost; my touch does not bring death."

He reached over and touched her cheek, then his fingers brushed the horse-skin cloak and he snatched them away as if burnt. The terrified awe had changed for something commoner. "But Gorliv was right, you've learned witchcraft."

Eysla set the girl down. "Not then. Not when he accused me. The skin-song was Ashóli's gift, and that came later."

I had been invisible to them since Eysla had taken her own form. Now all eyes turned to me.

"You witched my sister," Toral accused. When he faced his sister, love and fear had warred in his face. Toward me, there was no conflict.

And what was there to say? It was true. But somehow *she asked me to* seemed like a weak defense. I said, in Kaltaoven to Eysla, "We need to go."

But as I said it, Toral grabbed me, closing my mouth with his hand, saying, "No more witching!"

I had not yet mastered Laaki's skill of taking my skin without speaking the song aloud. I could do it now and again, but never, it seemed, when I had most need. I struggled against his grip, expecting Eysla to come to my aid, but she seemed frozen. Instead, Toral was the one who got help, as several of the men who had been watching the whole matter brought rope and rags to bind and gag me. At least they did not take my skin-cloak. Perhaps they didn't know enough to take it, or perhaps they thought me well enough restrained. Then they dragged me into the main hall of the largest house, scattering people from their tasks there, and thrust me into a chair. Then, with Eysla looking on, Toral set a knife to my throat and untied the gag.

"No strange tongues, no lies, no witching," he warned.

I tried to nod without cutting myself.

"Can you take this curse off my sister?" he asked.

"It isn't a curse," I answered thickly. I felt his hand tighten on the knife. "No lie!" I pleaded hastily. "She controls it. I only gave her the tools."

"It's true," Eysla added. Would he listen to her? "I asked her to witch Sunna's skin for me so that I could wear it. She never did anything to *me*."

"Then how do you explain what went on in the yard? That wasn't my sister—that was a wild beast! Eysla, what have you become?"

She shook her head in distress. "I'm still me."

He looked from one of us to the other. Mutters ran through the room, too low and strange for me to follow. Toral nodded to one of the men to gag me again and then the knife came away from my throat. He held his hand out to Eysla. "Give me the witch-skin."

She clutched it tighter around her. "Why?"

"I'll burn it, and then you'll be free of this. I won't have you bringing witchery here."

"No!" Eysla cried, but it seemed to have more of pleading than of defiance.

He cocked his head in confusion. "Eysla, why did you come home?"

I could hear her voice quaver as she answered, "I wanted to see you again—to see that all was well."

After a long moment, he held out his arms and she fell into them. I could see tears slowly tracking down her face, although she made no sound.

"Do you want to stay?" he asked. "No marriage, no Gorliv—everything just as it was?"

"I...I don't know," she answered.

"Stay. Stay for a bit, at least. You don't need this for now. You don't need to decide anything right now."

And as he spoke, he slipped the cloak slowly off her shoulders and gathered it up, folding it across his arm, before her in easy reach. And not until she nodded did he turn and take it out of the room. It was masterful. I could easily see how he turned out well-trained horses.

When he returned empty-handed, it was to deal with me. Eysla stood by me firmly now, but how long would that last? She made him promise I would come to no harm, but then neither would he set me free—not until she had made her choice. So I was returned to the room I had slept in, but this time there was a bar across the outside of the door and I was bound and gagged.

When they left me alone, I set my mind to my skin-song and, on the third or fourth try, managed to take on my skin but leave the bonds behind. What holds a woman is only a moment's tangle to a wildcat. But still there was the room, with no windows to squeeze through, not enough space for anything but a mouse to slip under the door, and not even anything much to hide in.

A mouse. Perhaps. It was worth a try. Eysla's family kept a tidy house, but there is no kitchen that doesn't have a mouse in it somewhere. Laaki had taught me how to call creatures to me. It was a skill she didn't care to practice—there is an unspoken pact we have with the creatures we use—but if there were ever a time it could be excused, this was it. I changed to my own skin once more and crooned the call softly so that the sound would not carry beyond the door, although the call itself would. Some minutes later, one came, squeezing itself through the sill and sniffing around for food. Trying not to startle it, I shifted to crooning my skin-song. Then I pounced.

It felt strange to sing the death-song for vermin, even just a token verse, but it would have felt stranger yet not to. The creature would lend me its skin and I would honor its death. They had taken my knife, so it was claw and tooth to skin the creature. And then there was the long task of discovering what the skin-song of a mouse would be. It was not an easy matter, but fear sharpens the wits, and Laaki had always said I was much quicker than most. If I had meant to wear a mouse-skin as a normal thing—what a strange thought—I would, of course, have gathered enough to make a proper cloak. But a single skin was enough for the task. The harder part was taking my cat-skin inside with me.

My plan had taken several hours, and I was just poking my nose under the door to see if the way were clear when footsteps came near with a rattle of dishes and the aroma of food. I dashed for the darkest corner of the room as the door swung open. There was a gasp, the smash of dropped crockery, and then the door slammed shut again. I wiggled under it and went in search of Eysla, but the house was filled with running and shouting and even as a mouse my limbs still ached and slowed me down. In the end, it seemed safer to find a quiet corner and wait for dark.

With the cover of night, I took to the grassy rooftops in cat-form, listening at doorways and windows for some clue to Eysla's whereabouts. At last my ears picked up her breathing—and occasionally something like a sob—coming through a small latticed window nearly hidden under the eaves. She was alone. The door opposite the window was closed and, I suspected, bolted. I could just barely squeeze through one of the lattice-openings. I begin to think that any size larger than a cat is inconvenient in a crisis. She looked up when I dropped to the floor and urgently laid a finger against her lips as I shed my skin. I glanced at the door and she nodded. I leaned close and whispered, "If you say the word, I will leave."

She shook her head and held me tightly. I hadn't realized how much I dreaded her answer until I got it. She whispered in turn. "I want my skin."

I pointed to the window and she nodded with a quizzical look. Now the problem. Which would frighten her less: forcing the mouse-form on her or taking her inside my skin? We had never shared the intimacy of two souls within a single body. I knew it could be terrifying and this was no time for panic. It must be the mouse-skin, then. She had to stifle a giggle when I pulled out the small coin-shaped pelt. I placed it on top of her head and mouthed the words of the skin-song. When she was changed, I lifted her up through the lattice, then drew my cat-skin about me and followed. I could feel her trembling when I touched her with my whiskers. *Don't go away—be Eysla*, I thought. If ever there were a time when the body's instincts warred with the mind, this was it: cat and mouse. I picked her up gently by the scruff of the neck and leapt up to the roof, from roof to wall, and from wall to outside the compound and into the fields.

When I thought we were a safe distance, I set her down in the grass and brought both of us to our proper shapes again. She took my hand and held it as if for her life. "Ashóli, are you hurt? Did he..."

I squeezed her fingers. "I'm well. Do you know where he put your skin? With any luck, we can be away tonight."

"Ashóli, wait." Eysla seemed to be struggling with something. "I don't want to leave—not like this. I just want my skin."

I pulled my hand from hers. "For what? So he can take it again? He'll put out his hand and you'll give him anything he asks for."

"I thought he was going to kill you!"

I followed that thought. "So, if I'm not there, you think it will be different?"

"Maybe. I don't know. I don't want to lose you, either."

What I was near to losing was my temper. "Make up your mind! You can be Kaltaoven or you can have your family. Not both. You have to choose."

"You don't have to make that choice," she said bitterly.

I thought she was being willfully stupid. "Do you want me to help you get your skin, or do you want me to leave now and never come back?"

"Ashóli, don't..."

"Don't what?"

I saw her face close down like a shuttered window. "Ashóli, will you help me get my skin-cloak back."

Relief again, but more uncertain this time. I nodded.

She crouched to clear a space of ground and draw a map by the light of the moon. "Toral must have it in his private room. That would be here." She sketched the layout of the main building. "There's a chest by his bed where he keeps valuables. That's one possibility."

"Locked?"

"Not usually, but tonight, who knows? He doesn't know what to expect."

"Does the room have windows? Even just a lattice like yours did?"

She thought a moment. "Yes, I think so. It's on the outside wall, at least. That would be here."

"Then we go in the same way we came out," I said, holding up the mouse-skin.

"One more thing," Eysla said hesitantly.

I looked back at the map, wondering where the difficulty came in. "Yes?"

"Could I ride somewhere other than your mouth?"

I laughed. "Now you know why there are skins we just don't sing! It would be a shame to have one's own kin for dinner by accident. There's another way we can do it." I had explained once about how I could take her inside my own skin—how she would be carried along passively, without senses or will to move, with only my mind for company. I offered her that choice.

I could tell she was shaken by the thought, but she nodded. I could feel her initial fear, and then her calm when I spoke to her in my mind and gave her an anchor in the void. As I slunk through the tall grasses back toward the settlement, I tried to feed her enough of what I saw and heard to distract her.

This is what it's like, she told me.

What?

When Sunna shares her skin with me—this is what it's like. Except that there is more of me and less of her. And she is still only a beast, with a beast's understanding. She speaks to me only in the way of a horse, but still she speaks.

I thought about that for the rest of my run. Was it only that she saw the matter in that way? Or was the wearing of skins different for her than it was for me and those who had taught me?

There was a window, with framed glass, not just an open lattice this time. The catch was on the inside but, by a miracle, it wasn't turned, only shut. I hooked claws in the frame and pulled it out, certain that even human ears must hear the sound. There was no one in the room. It seemed too lucky to be true. We slipped in and I released us both from the cat-skin. Eysla's cloak was in the chest, unlocked, as she had thought. She threw it around her shoulders and I saw a shudder of pleasure go through her. She had become truly Kaltaoven now; there was no doubt. Her skin was her spirit. I stepped closer to take us both under the cat-skin again when the door opened.

Toral stared at us for a moment, but with no surprise. "I had someone watching all around the house. If even an ant had entered, I would have known. So, Eysla, I suppose I have my answer."

"No, you don't," she began bluntly.

I wasted no time trying to untangle what she meant. We still had a chance of escape. I cast the cloak over the both of us with no warning and leapt out the window before Toral could stop us. There was a shout behind us, but it was drowned by the shout from within my mind. *Ashóli, let me out!* It wasn't a cry of trapped panic, but of furious anger. I was nearly tripped in my tracks by the force of it, and released us both from the skin simply to escape that anger.

Toral's men ringed us on all sides. Toral himself had come the long way around out of the house and approached. "Why?" he asked as he stopped some distance away and signaled his men to do the same. "You could have gotten away clean. Why?"

"How dare you!" Eysla said, burning him with the same anger she had turned on me. "How dare you take my life away from me with your 'choices'! Day or night; milk or water; red or blue; my family or my skin-cloak. Don't you understand? They are both a *part* of me. They aren't something I can choose to give up. You can steal my cloak from me, you can destroy it, and it will *still* be a part of me. And you," she continued, turning on me. "It's all so simple for you if all skin-wearers are Kaltaoven and all Kaltaoven are skin-wearers. I can speak your tongue, and sing your songs, and wear your gift, and I will never be one of you. Not in that way. And there is nothing you can offer me that will take the place of my family."

Nothing? I thought. *You haven't listened to what I want to offer.*

Eysla addressed us both now. "I don't accept the choices you set before me; I choose none of them. I will not go away and become dead again. I will not give up my skin." She took my hand. "I will not turn away from you. I could not bear to leave you. Give me different choices." Her words were pleading, but her voice held more of command.

A spark flared in my heart. There was a long, heavy stillness between us. Not silence, exactly, for there was a low stir and murmur from within the houses around the yard where people watched from every opening. I determined to speak first to prove...something, I wasn't sure what.

"Eysla?"

She turned toward me hesitantly.

"Eysla, I have been—I fear—something less than a teacher, but—I hope—something more than a friend. If you think there is more I can teach you, I would like the chance. And to lose you as a friend would tear my heart." I wanted to use a different word than friend. "But I cannot live among people who hate and fear me. That is not your choice, but mine."

She turned then toward her brother.

He spread his arms helplessly. "I never wanted anything but what was best for you. Where could you have had different choices?"

Eysla shook her head. "What was the choice when I married Gorliv? The choice to wait for the next man who offered? What was the choice when he accused me of killing my child? The choice to give up and die? Give me a better choice this time."

"Eysla, if it were only me... I have the whole family to consider."

Her face lost none of its stoniness. "You spoke for them freely enough before. Why hesitate now?"

He stared around him in the flickering light of the torches. Now *he* looked like the trapped animal. "What do you expect me to say? That you may come and go as you please, in whatever body you please, with whatever companions you please? This place and these people are my responsibility; I have no right to abandon that to you or anyone else."

"Do you trust me so little?" Eysla's expression might have softened somewhat, but it might have been a trick of the light. "No, I don't ask that. Just give me a choice we both can live with."

Toral drew himself together and crossed his arms, but he lacked the conviction he had shown before. "Then here is my choice. You may live here, under my rule and upon my support, and give up this witchery. Or you may maintain yourself as best you see fit and visit when you choose, as any of our kinsmen do, but only wearing your natural shape." He glanced over at me and added grudgingly, "and that goes for your companions, too. Will that do as a choice?"

"It will do for now," she answered. She turned to me and took me by the hand. I realized I was trembling, whether from relief or from the aches of my body that I had denied all day. Eysla felt it and frowned in concern. She said to Toral, "And since we are both in our own shapes, I presume we are welcome?"

"Eysla, no," I said softly. "I don't want—"

"Hush," she answered quickly. "You're in no shape to travel tonight. Maybe not tomorrow. Well, brother?"

He was not happy, but at last he shrugged and gestured back toward the house.

The moon shone brightly through the window of the room they gave us. A large window. One that opened. That had been *my* only demand. I yawned and said, "Perhaps a few days here won't go amiss after all."

As we curled up to share warmth in the large box-bed, Eysla touched the back of my neck and said, "Not too many days. I'm beginning to miss your fur already."

I gathered my courage. I had never offered her the chance to say yes or no to what I wanted. It was time to stop blaming her for that. "I would miss your skin." I used the Kaltaoven word that meant the fleshly skin and not a skin-cloak. I turned toward her and traced my finger across her cheek. "I would like to share that with you as well, if it is your choice."

Her breath caught and then she, too, reached out to cup my cheek. "I hoped...but I didn't know how to ask for that. I didn't know if you wanted—"

A "yes" should always be said with the mouth, but no words were involved when I did so.

The Skin Trade

Looking back, the moment I walked through the gates of Wilentelu, I set my feet on the trail that reunited me with Laaki and my family. I would have laughed at the thought then, because we stayed in Wilentelu far longer than we ever intended.

We came there to deliver horses. Eysla's brother Toral had made a contract with the Marchalt of Wilentelu and because Eysla and I had never traveled in that direction before, we were more than willing to take the offered chance. Toral and I had come a fair distance since our first meeting. Then, I was the witch who had bespelled his sister. Well, and by his eyes it was true. I made the skin-song for Eysla's dead mare that let her wear it and run four-footed across the hills. We Kaltaoven don't think of that as witchery any more than you would think that of fire or of language itself. But in the face of his sister's determination, he retreated by small steps: first, not to kill me; then, to allow us within his clan's lands but only in human shape. Then, one day last winter, when the need was great, he had begged us to put on our skin-cloaks, when only those bodies could best serve. I counted it a victory when, at last, his only remaining grudge was that I was his sister's lover and he'd had no part in bargaining a contract.

Now there were horses to deliver at a long distance, and Toral had no more doubts about asking us to take them than if he had done it himself. For once, Eysla and I approached a new town riding side by side, instead of Eysla wearing her skin to carry both me and our belongings. I'd had no experience with horses until I met Eysla, and no experience riding except with her. I had to learn everything new on this trip.

My teacher, Laaki, had told stories of the stone-built cities in the north, but I'd never truly believed that many people could all live in the same place. When we first saw Wilentelu at a distance, it was just a collection of walls and roofs on a rocky rise that stood out from the broad green river valley. Between our vantage and those buildings lay immense grain fields spotted with smaller buildings and streaked with dusty roads. Then we rode all morning and the town grew nearer only slowly. I began to understand how ill-fitting even the word "town" was for this place. What had seemed a little river turned into a wide but sluggish flood and the horses balked at the crossing until Eysla lost patience and sang her cloak about her to lead them across. She had finally learned the trick of taking our baggage in under her skin as well, so we made the crossing dry. A rest on the far bank gave us the chance to repack our gear, stow our skin-cloaks away, and to brush the horses into a more impressive show. No harm in making sure the Marchalt knew he was getting full value. Three riders from the city met us halfway from the riverbank—wiry, compact men on horses that made me understand why they had searched so far to find better. They shouted orders at us and at each other in a thick version of Eysla's native tongue, and together we gathered the herd into a rough pen set against the city wall. When the gate was closed at last, the first of them nodded briefly in our direction then turned back to watch the horses mill and circle in the pen. It was clear he thought he had dismissed us. I moved back into his path. "Forgive my discourtesy, but we were told to deliver them to the Marchalt himself."

He looked me up and down as if only noticing me for the first time. "You have." And then as an afterthought, "Come to the Shalen later for your payment." Then it was clear he had no more attention to give us, so we gathered up our bags and set off around the curve of the walls towards the main gate. They were built in a warm yellow sandstone that was only just beginning to soften around the edges. It had glowed like gold from a distance. But the walls were thick and high—meant for some hard purpose—and the guards who stopped us at the gate questioned us closely, even though our purpose must have been obvious. If we wanted to sell goods, we must pay a fee at the guildhall; when we found lodging, we must register at the Shalen; before we left, we must have permission from the Marchalt. Fees and payments were all new to me, though Eysla seemed to understand it all. The lands I'd traveled in dealt in trade and bargaining, but here they used metal coins and one must know the value of each. We entered with our heads whirling. If I had been alone, I might have turned back, but we needed to collect payment for the horses and Eysla gave me the courage to continue. And I must confess I was curious to see what lay within.

The wonder was worth it. Even more than my own memories, I remember watching Eysla take it all in. Walking through the streets of Wilentelu was like galloping in horse-skin across rough ground: exciting, with new sights rushing past wherever you looked. Every moment you think you can't continue at that pace, but you never want to stop.

"Ashóli," she whispered to me. "Where do they all live? How do they feed them all?"

And then we came out from a canyon made by two buildings into an open, stone-floored field and there was the answer: people selling every kind of food, and more.

"We may leave with all the trade goods we brought," I grumbled. We were more used to small villages hungry for anything from outside. Even more, we were used to being obvious strangers and stared at, but here no one seemed to notice us, and we did all the staring. Perhaps everyone was a stranger to them; I saw people from every land we'd traveled through, and more that we hadn't.

We tired of walking—or rather, of carrying all our goods—before we tired of looking, and asked the way to the guildhall as we'd been told. And once we'd paid our fees from the coins Toral had sent with us and been told the rules of when and where we could sell, we were directed to a house with rooms available, by chance belonging to a cousin of the guildhall clerk.

"I want to do nothing but sleep!" Eysla said, testing out the first real bed we'd seen since leaving her family's home.

I sorted out the bundle of our spare clothes from the goods we carried to sell. "We need to find this Shalen first. At the gate they said we need to tell them where we're staying, and I want to collect that fee while the Marchalt still remembers he owes it."

Eysla groaned and sat up. "Both of us?"

I focused very carefully on smoothing out our clean garments. "I'd rather we stayed together."

She heard in my voice what I tried to conceal. "It's all so strange, but do you think there's any danger? "

I shrugged. "I don't know. I just... I'd rather not be separated for now."

She took my hand and stood up. "But at least let me fetch some water to wash."

And because there seemed no reason not to, among such exotic sights, and because it made for a finer display, we took our skin-cloaks with us, as well as wearing our best clothes. Sometimes we were more cautious. Laaki had tried to teach me to be wary of all strangers and assume there were enemies everywhere, and I could understand why she felt that way, given what she had seen. But I had Eysla as an argument on the other side, and all the people on our travels who had not cared—or not known—what the cloaks meant. It seemed to me that if you did not put on or cast off a skin-shape in front of people, they were mostly content to let you be. And we had survived the few exceptions well enough.

Shalen, as we understood, meant "king's house", but the Marchalt was not the king; he only led the king's soldiers in Wilentelu and collected the fees and kept watch for raids. It seemed an awkward way to live, to have a clan so wide that you might only see your leader once in the year. Strange as well to have people whose only work was to carry weapons. But in every town, they said, there was a Shalen, not simply for the king to live in when he passed through, but so those who were his eyes and hands would stand under his roof and so in his authority. It stood near the center of the city, or so I guessed, and the sandstone had been covered by a smoother, harder face, with veins of color. The first room we entered was like a stone forest, with the roof held high above our heads by tall columns. At the far end, raised up, stood an empty chair, and then a smaller chair before it to one side. But it, too, was empty. People came and went along the aisles to either side and, just as in the market square, they took no notice of us until we asked the way.

I think I had expected to see the Marchalt himself, but it was a quiet, piercing-eyed clerk who gave us the money and had us mark his book and then took the information on our lodgings. But as we left, the head man was sitting in the side chair in the main hall, talking to a group of people. He looked up to see us passing and sent a guard to bring us close while he dismissed the others.

"You're Keltowin," he said abruptly, pointing to my cloak.

It took me a moment to untangle his pronunciation. "Yes," I said hesitantly. "I am Kaltaoven, a skin-wearer. We—" I shot a glance at Eysla. It was too complicated to explain the full story. "We are."

"You should have told me. I like to know these things."

He didn't seem angry; he only said it as a fact, but my heart was racing and every sense was alert to what lay between us and the door. "We didn't know," I stammered. "Forgive—"

He made a dismissive gesture. "What shapes do you wear? No, let me guess." He reached out to finger my cloak and I tried not to flinch back. "A forest cat and," he glanced at Eysla, "a horse. A pity. I might have had work for you if it were something more useful. There's a bird-man lives off by the east gate who carries messages to Mergenel for me, but a cat's not much practical use and real horses serve as well as magic ones."

I think I was struck dumb for several moments. I had known people who feared us or envied us, and even one or two who thought we were gods, but I'd never heard us taken so much for granted. "Bird-man" indeed. Eysla filled the gap.

"We regret there is no service we can do for you."

He waved off the apology once more. "A pity," he repeated. "I sometimes think what I could do with an entire troop of your people. To combine the best skills of men and beasts..." He shook his head. "But Keale says there are few of you in these lands, and too far scattered."

When we had first set out on our travels together, Eysla might have blurted out the truth—that I could sing skins for anyone, as I had for her, and not only for my own people. And then I would have had to make excuses and we would have quarreled. She had learned the value of secrets since then. And I had come to the truth of Laaki's accusations: that I had sung a skin for Eysla to show off my own power, to impress her, and to prove that I could. There was more to being Kaltaoven than wearing a cloak and taking on its beast-shape. That wasn't a temptation I cared to offer a stranger.

And so we were dismissed and had nothing to worry us but sleeping in comfort until well into the next morning.

But when we rose finally and had eaten, rather than searching out a place in the market to begin selling, I suggested that we explore the city further—beginning with the east gate.

"To find Keale?" Eysla asked.

I nodded.

"Perhaps you would rather go alone."

"What's this nonsense?" I demanded. "Do you think I plan to abandon you for the first Kaltaoven I meet since I left home?"

She shrugged but didn't meet my eyes.

"Don't be silly. You're my skin-daughter, my road-sister, and my heart. Birth couldn't make you any closer than you are already. Do I worry every time we visit your family that you'll shed your skin and leave me?"

She tilted her head and smiled sideways at me. "Yes."

I laughed. "Be fair! Not since that first time, and confess that you gave me reason!"

Then she stood and threw her cloak around her and kissed me. "The east gate, then, and a man we've never met who may or may not be wearing a feathered cloak."

But as it turned out, the search was short. The east gate market was for goods from far foreign lands: cloth and spices, fine jewelry and rough gems, songbirds and strange written things. And just when I was ready to begin asking where the man named Keale lived, I looked down between two hampers of small furs—ermine, sable, and miniver—and sitting in a wicker tray was a small, intricately-carved wooden bowl of a design my cousins made. Then I looked up into the pleasantly plain face of a woman, framed by a collar of soft gray fox fur, who was staring with equal intensity at my own cloak.

I scrambled for the words for a moment. Eysla and I spoke the Kaltaoven tongue between us all the time, but the last time

I had addressed someone in the formal mode was when Laaki was newly come to our village.

She, I think, had the same difficulty, and stammered out a response at last as Eysla wandered over from the next stall to join us. The small child at the woman's side had no such difficulty and cheerfully cried out a family greeting, only to be shushed and corrected for being too familiar.

"I think you must know Keale," I said, as Eysla murmured her own formal greeting. "The Marchalt mentioned his name yesterday when we arrived," I added quickly when her face tightened in suspicion.

"My husband is at home working," she answered. And then after a slight pause, "Perhaps you will join us for a meal at mid-day?"

"If it's no burden to you," I responded.

Eysla took the carved bowl from me and turned it over in her hands. The woman switched into market-patter. "It's a fine bowl—well-made and beautiful. Brought at great expense all the way from Karskar. Perhaps it reminds you of home?"

I had to laugh. "More than you know! But it hasn't come anywhere near as far as from Karskar. There's my cousin Goalnen's mark on the bottom."

A bright eagerness came into her face. "Your cousin? Then you—" She broke off. "It isn't the appropriate time for questions. But you will come? We live down the fountain lane." She gestured towards a narrow street by the public well at one side of the square. "Near the end, with the red door. We...oh, never mind, if you'll help me carry these things we can go now."

And so, in the end, we gathered her wares back into their hampers and followed her bemusedly to the house with the red door.

When he had been fetched out of the back workshop, Keale greeted us with the same bright eagerness. "We don't get many Kaltaoven passing through, and most are far-wanderers like we were. There are few settled clans in reach of the Wilen—none in easy distance."

And as we were settled onto cushions in the main room, and plied with food and drink, their story emerged. Keale and Haalan had each left their families, intending it only for a wander-season, but they had lost touch. Keale's family had migrated on, and if they had left signs for him to follow, those had been lost by the time he returned. Haalan's had fled before attackers and she dared not try to follow in case she betrayed them. But the years had cast them both up in Wilentelu and they had found each other.

"It's been a good home," Haalan said. "The Marchalt is a hard man, but he values the service Keale can do for him, and we have been under his protection." There was an edge in her voice that I couldn't sort out yet. "But lately we've been hoping to return to our people, or find a clan to join. Vék is old enough to start wearing a skin, and we have another to come." She laid her hand briefly on her belly. "And they won't find skins here in Wilentelu."

I shot a warning glance over at Eysla and she nodded in understanding. Almost certainly I would offer to sing skins for their children, but I wanted to hear the whole story first. "But you trade with my people," I said. "It's a far distance, but not too far if you have the reason to travel it."

Keale shook his head. "We deal with a trader. People will pay more for Kaltaoven goods if you wear a skin-cloak even if you bought the goods from another, which benefits us both. But the trader won't tell us anything of where he travels—he's afraid we'd cut him out of the bargain. And even if we knew—"

"He wouldn't let you go," Eysla broke in.

I looked at her in surprise. "Who?" The other two clearly knew what she meant.

"The Marchalt," Eysla said. "He does more than value your service, I'd guess; he depends on it. And he doesn't seem the sort to give up something he depends on."

Haalan nodded. "Oh, it's always couched in soft terms. 'It's not convenient at this season, we'll talk about it later.' and 'There's no sense leaving until you have some place to go. Let me see what I can discover about these traders for you.' And somehow the seasons turn again. He has us watched."

"I think you're wrong there," Keale said, but she hushed him with an angry glance.

"We might be able to leave the city if we were careful, but we can't travel quickly or quietly with Vék. If he wanted to fetch us back, his soldiers would find us before the next dawn." Her voice grew bitter.

"And what do you want from us?" Eysla asked. I grabbed her arm to warn her but she shook me off. "No, Ashóli. I know it's horribly bad manners to ask such things directly, but we need to know. Why do you trust us with all this when you barely know our names? What do you think we can do to help, and what danger will it bring?"

"I should think we could trust other skin-wearers," Haalan began, then she turned away and started crying. Keale threw up his hands helplessly as the child began bawling in response and I calculated that our welcome was wearing thin.

"You've given us a great deal to think about," I said. "Perhaps tomorrow we could offer you an evening meal and we can talk further? We're staying at the House of the Lilies near the Guildhall. May we expect you then?"

Keale nodded with a wry but grateful smile. "We will come."

We talked about it, Eysla and I, that evening when we'd had our fill of exploring the city. I'd expected her to argue more for their side, but for once she was the more cautious.

"There's more to this than helping them escape a trap. This man has power here and a long reach—longer than just to the next village. If we trick the Marchalt to help them flee, then we can't stay either, and I want more time to taste this place. And what if he takes his revenge on my brother's bargain? There's still the second half of the price to be paid in grain, and the promise of more dealings in the future. This isn't life and death where we need to snatch any way out that offers. There's room for bargaining here."

"Bargaining..." I echoed, thinking about the possibilities. "I wish Laaki were here. No one else I know can craft a bargain like she can." She'd taught me how far bargaining could stretch when she bought my death and sold my life back to me.

Eysla smiled. She'd heard the story often enough, although there were parts I'd rather forget. "What sort of bargain would she make?"

"Oh, something complex and interwoven that leaves everyone thinking they've gotten the best of everyone else. I don't have that skill. Even you're better at it than I am." But that gave me ideas, and we talked for a long time about what Keale and Haalan might want, and what the Marchalt might want, and what we might gain between them.

We tried our hand as merchants the next day. The crowded market was a hard place to sell. People wanted to be coaxed, cajoled, seduced into considering the possibility that they might have a use for our goods. The prices they were willing to pay—and in coin, not trade—were startling, though I was only beginning to think in that type of value. By the afternoon, we were both enjoying ourselves and there was a promise of high gains, though hard won.

We packed our goods early to have time to collect the makings of a meal together before the food market closed as well, but when we returned to the House of Lilies, a group of the Marchalt's men were waiting for us and would say nothing to our questions but that we were wanted in the Shalen. So we followed, hoping that the empty room and abandoned food would tell the necessary tale.

We needn't have worried. Keale and Haalan were there before us, standing rigid in the hall before the Marchalt's chair. Vék was in a corner being entertained with a game of sticks by one of the guards.

Haalan looked like she might spit when she saw us. She advanced as far as the guards would allow her and said, "You betrayed us!" Her husband laid a hand on her shoulder and whispered something in her ear, but she shook him off. "You betrayed all our secrets, but I know secrets of yours to tell."

"Which secrets would those be?" I asked. I wasn't going to guess and give away more than they might have already.

The Marchalt had been watching us from his chair with an expression that was impossible to read. But when he raised his hand and pointed at me everyone else fell back and was silent. "Perhaps," he said, "it would be better if you told us what secrets you have to be known. I told you before: I like to know these things."

Eysla's hand slipped into mine and tightened. We'd discussed this the night before. One thing we might bargain for with him was knowledge, but not if he thought he was bargaining. This was a man comfortable with his own power and accustomed to being obeyed. He might reward something freely given, but he wouldn't pay for something he thought he was owed. I took half a step forward and bowed.

"I am a *byal-dónen*, a skin-singer. I can take the skins of beasts and make a song for them so one of our people can wear the skin. I can wear any skin I choose. It's not a skill we all have." I gestured towards Keale and Haalan. "They needed a skin-cloak for their son to wear and for the child to come. This evening I was going to bargain with them for the cloaks."

I could tell from the surprised look on Keale's face and the expectant look of the Marchalt that this wasn't the secret they had expected to hear. That left only one. I looked back at Eysla, since it was hers to tell.

She stepped forward to stand beside me and said, "I'm not born Kaltaoven—it's no secret." She gazed coolly at Haalan. "My tongue and my face make it plain enough to anyone who is and the Marchalt has traded with my brother for years."

The Marchalt rose from his chair. "And yet you wear one of these skin-cloaks. For show or for use?"

I could see that it crossed her mind to show him, but she only said, "For use."

His eyes widened as if he hadn't believed that would be the answer. He looked over at me, "Your work?" I nodded. "How is it possible? I was told... Did you lie to me?" he asked Keale.

"It isn't done," I said quickly. "It's forbidden. I broke the rules."

"Then you can break them again," he said confidently. He gestured to the soldiers who stood by Keale's family. "They can go, but not outside the city walls. Not until this is finished." And they left, without looking back at us. Keale, I think, because he was ashamed, and Haalan because she was afraid.

Haalan was right: he couched everything in soft words. There was never a time when he said, "Do this, or that will happen," or commanded anything directly. But we soon came to understand that life would be very convenient and pleasant if certain things came to pass that he desired. And then he let us go. It was masterful—he would have been a match even for Laaki, and I had only a fraction of her skills in that field.

When we were alone again in our room, we spoke only briefly of leaving. I could take the skin of a night-bird and sing it around the both of us and all our goods for long enough to escape beyond his reach. But all the same arguments remained. We were thoroughly tangled in this tapestry now: by Toral and the horses, by Keale's son and his hope for a skin-cloak, even by that mythical loyalty that I was supposed to share with all Kaltaoven. Like Eysla, I wanted more of a taste of this place. I didn't want to lose the choice of returning. And, strangely enough, I liked the Marchalt. What he wanted was impossible, but I could understand why he wanted it. He'd had a taste of how useful we Kaltaoven could be: messages delivered at the speed of birdflight; sentries with eyes and ears beyond what any enemy could manage. To him, we squandered our skills. To us, wearing a skin wasn't a tool, it was what we are.

We didn't sleep well that night, but we slept.

In the morning, we didn't wait for soldiers to fetch us; we went to the Shalen as soon as people were stirring in the streets. There we waited, as whispers ran around us, until the Marchalt appeared.

I told him about the three-fold bargain. "It's a...a ritual we Kaltaoven have, to make ties between families. Three exchanges proposed and accepted. Not marketplace exchanges, but something of deeper value."

He looked amused. "And you would propose one of these triple bargains with me?"

I shook my head. "It's not something for outsiders." I wondered, even as I said it, why not? Could someone not Kaltaoven understand how sacred such a bargain was? I pushed the thought away. "With your permission I would like to propose a three-fold bargain with Keale and Haalan."

He was still amused; I counted on that. So he sent for the others to be brought to join us. And when they came, hesitant and nervous, I spread my skin-cloak there on the stone floor of the hall and sat on it to chant the opening call for the three-fold bargain.

They looked at each other, then at the Marchalt, then Keale shrugged and spread his own cloak to sit. He had nothing to lose. He could refuse the bargain, if he chose, with no shame attached.

It was an awkward bargaining. The formal phrases didn't come as easily in a language the Marchalt could understand, but he was my target, and it was unlikely he'd be willing for us to bargain in the Kaltaoven tongue in his presence. "Here is my first offer," I said, "that I will make a skin-song, as you choose, for your son, and in exchange you will give me your contract with the traders to the east."

Keale considered silently for a moment. "It is a fair bargain," he said at last. "But I cannot answer yet. Without those trading contracts we would need to find a new way to live. My work for the Marchalt is not enough to support us."

I nodded and continued. "Here is my second offer. I will make a skin-song for the child to come, and in exchange you will give me your rights to your house and workshop."

I think he saw, then, the hope of a way out, but he protested the exchange. "The child is yet unborn and anything may befall." He made a sign to avert bad luck. "The house and workshop have solid value. But trading contracts, like an unborn child, are a promise only. Reverse the exchanges and I will consider it fair."

I nodded again and felt my heart begin to race in anticipation. "Here is my third offer. I have rights in a clan for which I have no need." (It was the simple truth; a skin-singer would be welcome back, clan-right or no.) "You have the trust and dependence of a man of power and importance. Will you exchange that for my clan-right?"

I could hear the Marchalt stirring behind me but I dared not look. Keale stared past me, searching for some sign of what to answer. At last he said, "It seems an unfair exchange. That trust and dependence have become a burden to me, but you offer me something of great value for it. For my part, I would accept, but you ask for something that is not mine to give."

I heard the Marchalt's voice behind me. "And she can wear any skin? Not just the one? Keale, I have never kept you here against your will. I never refused you permission to leave." But he had discouraged the question, I was certain.

Keale swallowed visibly. "If the Marchalt is willing to give you his trust and rely on your skills, then I gladly surrender them to you. Is the bargain well-made?"

"*Gyel-dón a-don*," I said. "It is well-made."

He rose and took up his skin-cloak again, then waited to see what would come next. I rose too and turned at last to face the Marchalt. As always, his face was hard to read. I had committed myself to serve this man for some time to come and I wanted badly to know more of what went on behind that face.

"What bargain will you make with me?" he asked at last.

"The bargain is yours to offer," I countered. I wanted to hear from his own mouth what he thought he could ask for.

"You will carry my messages as a bird—you can take that form?"

I nodded. "But you needn't bargain for that, it's yours already."

"And you can make a charm for anyone—anyone at all—to become a beast as you do?"

"I can sing the skin," I answered, "but it isn't so easy to wear it." I nodded in Eysla's direction where had been waiting, the more tense for not having a part to play. "When her skin was new, she sometimes lost herself in the beast. If you give a man a skin and he forgets himself, he may never come back. Which of your men is willing to risk that?"

He looked around the room, weighing them. "My men would do much for me." But I saw no volunteers and neither did he. It was one thing to watch witchery unfold in front of you; it was another to have it worked on you.

I knew then where to place my shot. "Would you order a man to do what you would not do yourself?"

For the first time that morning, I saw him smile broadly. "You drive a hard bargain indeed. But my own life isn't mine to risk, it's pledged to my king. Is the danger so great?"

I shrugged. "If I put the skin on you, I can take it off. A taste, if you like. It's safe enough unless you go mad in the first moment."

He shifted in his chair. I had pushed too far. He could not afford to back away now. Abruptly, he headed past me towards the door and snapped his fingers for all of us to follow. In the center of the courtyard he turned to me. "What shape will you give me?"

"Now?" I looked around. "I can only use the skins that are here." But before he could make a choice, Keale came forward and offered his cloak. It wasn't the one I would have picked. A natural falcon is a crazy bird. Beautiful and noble, but completely insane. If I left enough of the bird in the skin to carry him, would it be more than he could handle? Wasn't that what I wanted? To frighten him? But if he took flight there was no easy way to bring him back.

To my relief, he shook his head. "The horse, I think, if your friend will lend it."

Eysla wasn't happy about it, but I could see that she agreed with the choice. If he went mad, it was the one skin that would be easy to retrieve. So she slung it off from around her shoulders and placed it around his. I could see him steeling himself, and before he could lose his nerve I whispered, "Wear thy skin!"

His body blurred and stretched as he fell to all fours. There was a clatter of hooves as he danced backwards. His horse-body gave away what his human face would not. His ears were back and the whites of his eyes showed. He wheeled away, half-rearing as if trying for a human posture again, and then circled the courtyard, starting at every movement around him. Then, snorting and dancing, he came back to me. His ears were still back but he bent his head in a nod. I whispered the words that took the skin off him once more and we all pretended not to watch while he composed himself. When he handed the cloak back to Eysla he looked at her in new respect. I could see there were questions he wanted to ask later.

But at last he shook his head. "No, that would not be such a good idea, I think. Such power... A man who gets a taste for that would no longer make a good soldier. And a man with no taste for the change would be no use at all as a beast." I couldn't tell how much of that was honest and how much was to save face, but it didn't matter. We had come to a truce without my refusal or his retreat. The bargain was well-unmade.

He caused no further trouble for Keale and his family. They left a few days later, not from fear that he would change his mind, but because the child would not delay its coming for their comfort. We gave them a map—as best we could draw it—and instructions that would lead them true. They would arrive in enough time. I sent a message and a token for Laaki to tell her of the bargain and let her know I was well.

The next year, when the traders came over the mountains in the spring, bringing the furs and carvings my cousins had collected through the winter, they brought Laaki's message in return. That was when I knew that we would see each other again someday, though I couldn't imagine myself returning to stay. Like Eysla, I would need to weave new and different ties with my kin. And for now, I had bound myself to Wilentelu until we forged a different bargain. For now, we were content. Eysla was busy training her brother's horses and arranging to sell others. There was time and more for everything we might plan.

Skin and Bones

When the Marchalt of Wilentelu summoned me, I came—not for fear, but because I had bound myself to his service for a time. And when the Marchalt asked a question, he was used to being answered quickly. But I hesitated when he asked if I knew anything of a village of skin-changers five days ride north-west through the hills.

"You know I mean no harm to your people," he said sharply when the pause had grown too long.

I answered as carefully as I ever did. "Harm or not, if they don't care to be found by outsiders, it isn't my secret to share. But truth to tell, I don't know of one. There have been a few Kaltaoven from time to time in the marketplace, but it isn't polite to ask after their homes if they don't offer. Hard experience has made us cautious. Sometimes even we find each other only by rumor."

He gave a bark of laughter. "Come. Walk with me away from all...these." He waved his hand to take in the guards and servants, clerks and waiting officers who always buzzed around him in the Shalen—his hall of office—like bees in a hive. Then he led me out into a private garden where the only buzzing bees were in the flowers.

It was a hot day so I slipped the cloak of wildcat fur off my shoulders and draped it across my arm.

"Are you never without that?" the Marchalt asked teasingly. It had become a joke between us.

"I never know when you may need my services," I joked back. And then more seriously, "It reminds them—" I nodded back toward the hall. "—who I am. That I am your skin-singer, your Kaltaoven witch."

He grunted in acknowledgment then went straight to his business. "When I was new to the king's service—twenty years back or more, long before I was made Marchalt—I was given the task to survey the extent of the king's lands in Anwella."

He waved in the direction of the hills that reached up to the west and north where the Wilen itself turned south. Beyond them the mountains rose even higher in rocky peaks.

"My quarter was from the uplands that overlook the river, back as far into the unknown lands as the king's hand might reach. And on that survey, I came across a village of skin-changers, of Keltowin." He had never learned to say our name correctly. "They laughed at the thought that the king in Mergenel might have a say over their lives. I may have been a green puppy but I had the sense to laugh with them. But that was when I first had the idea..."

He gestured at me, or more accurately, at my skin-cloak.

"There was an old man, Emeen his name was—the one who put the magic in their skin-cloaks. He asked for stories of the wider world and gathered the children around to hear them. Now, it wasn't as if I'd traveled the world myself, but I could tell stories. And I thought, if I could have two of these people in every company of soldiers, I could... Well, best not to speak too loudly. But I asked if any wanted to follow me into the king's service and see more than their little sweep of hills. There were one or two who might have, I think, but nothing came of it at the time. We had stayed too long already. But when we left, the old man whispered to me that if he were thirty years younger and free to choose..."

The Marchalt shrugged. "But he was their only skin-singer, and his duty bound him."

He stared at nothing for a moment then shook his head. "I always hoped I'd planted a seed there, but who was I? Not even a captain of my own troop yet and no one to be listened to. When the king put the keeping of Wilentelu into my hands, I tried to find them, but the village was deserted and we didn't have the luck of stumbling across them again. But you, perhaps, will make better luck."

"What message would you have me take?" I asked hesitantly.

"Ashóli, this is nothing against your service. I have no complaints. But I've grown too used to having skin-changers around. Someday the road will call you back—you and your companion—and it will be easier for me to let you go if there are others to take your place."

I couldn't help but be reminded of those who had come before me in his service and the bargain I'd had to strike to convince him to let them leave. It hadn't escaped my notice that somehow it was never convenient for Eysla and me to leave the city at the same time.

"You know my needs well enough," he continued. "You know what I expect and what I offer. Find them. Tell them, and see if any are interested." He didn't need to add that, if I were persuasive enough, my own interests would be served as well.

"How long will you be gone this time?" Eysla asked me sleepily after the candles had been blown out that night.

"Not long. Two, three weeks. I suppose it depends on whether they are hiding or if they've simply drifted elsewhere. And it will depend on how they listen to the Marchalt's offer. I don't think he expects anyone to return with us at once, just to listen and consider."

"Us?"

I sighed. "That is what will slow me down. He's sending two of his men with me—not guards, I think, just other eyes and ears. But that means we'll travel at a horse's pace."

Eysla snorted in mock insult.

I had to laugh. "Your brother may breed fast horses, but wings are faster across hilly land. So until he breeds horses with wings, I'll call them slow."

She was silent for a moment, but I knew better than to think she was angry. "Ashóli," she asked. "How many are there? How many Kaltaoven?"

I propped myself up on one elbow to look at her in the faint moonlight. "Why?"

"I know your clan. And Laaki, your teacher, and her adopted sons. But their families are dead or lost. And the family whose place we took here. And this village of the Marchalt's. But that isn't very many. So many places we've been where they'd never heard of skin-changers. What if…?"

A shiver ran through me as I counted along with her list, but it passed. "You forget my mother's kin—she was a stranger to my clan. I've never met them but they're out there somewhere. Laaki's people are somewhere far to the east. And here in Wilentelu there have been a few Kaltaoven travelers. More than the Marchalt's men know about. With our skin-cloaks packed away we look enough like anyone else. And what's more—" I stroked her nose in the way I always did when teasing. "—if there weren't enough interesting strangers showing up from time to time, why, we'd all have to fall in love with *sálen*, with ordinary humans, like I did."

But Eysla's words rode with me in the days that followed as we made our way over hillside tracks and stony fords, following the Marchalt's careful map. Back at home, secrecy had been an unquestioned habit, but since I'd left on my wanderings, I'd grown less cautious and had taken little hurt from it. It was different for Eysla and me. Having no village and family to take care for, we could slip away and run if we needed. Laaki told darker stories of jealousy, greed, and fear, and what could happen when you'd put your heart into a house of stone and your children were hostages to the turning of fate. Today I had the Marchalt's protection, and if there were people in Wilentelu who feared me enough to harm me, they feared him more. But what of tomorrow? I'd seen enough of the king's court in Mergenel on my errands to know that not every *talodesh* had a Marchalt of similar mind.

When we found the overgrown foundations of the village's clan-hall and traced the ghosts of old fields in the pattern of the meadows I put away my favored cat-skin cloak and took out a cloak of falcon's feathers. Halkun and Kers had hobbled the horses to graze and begun to make camp but they stopped to watch me change. A skilled skin-singer can put on any skin without needing to know its song, but I chanted one anyway. It made for a better show.

"*Kael-keol i'éle i'óe,*
"*Yetaovog v'tev.*"

In the end, it took four days to find the new village: one for each point of the compass, with no luck until the last. I saw no signs that they had tried to hide it. Indeed, the northern edge of their planted lands lay along a travelers' track continuing further up into the hills and beyond. Clearly they had no objection to visitors, as such, so I returned to collect Halkun and Kers before making myself known to them.

It was a larger village than the one I had grown up in. I counted maybe forty buildings besides the large clan-hall. And an even more welcome difference from my childhood home was the crowd of children who swarmed out to meet us. Each one of a proper age wore a well-crafted skin-cloak. New. None of the fading and roughness that spoke of hoarded family heirlooms. I remembered too well the meanness that was bred by the lack of a *byal-dónen*'s skills.

The children were followed at a dignified distance by a group of five men and women, and it was to them that I made my courtesy.

"My name is Ashóli of a clan far to the east near Ganasset, but I come as the messenger of the Marchalt of Wilentelu, as do these men." I introduced my companions who were bearing patiently with not understanding a single word.

One of the older men stepped forward. He wore a cloak of cinnamon-colored bear skin and he introduced himself as Laeno. "I wondered if we would see you here someday."

When he spoke, I recognized him. He was one of those who had entered the city gates with his cloak hidden in his baggage. For that reason, I hadn't claimed an acquaintance at the time, although our eyes had met and recognized our kinship. "An invitation would have brought me sooner," I said, trying to convey respect for their privacy rather than reproach. "The Marchalt remembers this clan with friendship from when he was a young man. And he honors the memory of the *byal-dónen* you had at that time. He gave the name as Emeen, but I fear his tongue isn't skilled with our language and he may have meant Amyen." I hesitated in confusion as sharp glances darted between them. One man turned so pale I thought he might be sick. Clearly I had trodden on a sore toe, but how, I couldn't guess. I pressed on with what seemed a safe compliment, nodding towards the children. "My compliments to your current skin-singer, I can see the signs of great skill. I hope that I will be allowed to pay my respects while I am here."

"That may not be possible," Laeno said in a closed voice. "But we can offer you food and warm beds, and we will listen to the words of your Marchalt."

That first evening, as their custom dictated, we were fed and entertained but business was set aside. The next day word went out to those farther afield and there was more of a true feast in the clan-hall for all who gathered. The words the Marchalt had sent were fairly few; I was the message he wanted them to hear. So I told stories of the errands and tasks I was sent on, of the types of work that made a Kaltaoven valuable to a man with power.

"And what is he like, this Marchalt?" they asked. "Does he deal fairly?"

I'd been expecting the question, but was still groping for an answer. I couldn't say that I trusted him, other than to be what he was. We had come to be on easy terms, but I knew their limits. But there was one thing my people understood. "He will drive the hardest bargain that he can," I said at last. "But he will not break it once it is made." I could hear sounds of approval and see a few nods.

It seemed, in the end, that the Marchalt's errand might come to bear fruit. But on one point I was still waiting. The *byal-dónen* had not come to this gathering with the others. I'd looked closely around the hall and seen no one that they gave that deference to. In telling my tales they had learned that I shared the skill to sing power into skins. If I held them to the oldest customs, it would be an insult for me to be refused a meeting. Yet it was curiosity, not pride, that made me ask again, only to be met by the same prickly pushing aside of the matter.

The next day we settled down to more ordinary business. The Marchalt's men had brought gifts, politely disguised as goods to trade, and I left them playing bargaining games with a few of the Kaltaoven who shared enough of their speech to play. For my part, I put on feathers and was shown more of the lands they had made their own in this wilderness. Then there was time to speak more closely with a few of the younger men and women who thought it might be worth some years of exile to see more of the world before settling down. More than one questioned me about other clans, other wanderers. There was more than one soft glance thrown in my direction. It was not only adventure that might lure them into strange lands.

I asked again that evening if I might pay my respects to their skin-singer. We would be leaving in the morning and my curiosity was now an itch. Again I received an answer that was not an answer and I lay awake that night chewing on my mystery. At length I gave up on sleeping and put on my cat-skin against the cold and padded out along the moonlit path, enjoying the scents and sounds my human senses could not catch.

The sounds of an argument caught my ear, and I would have gone another way but someone was speaking of their *byal-dónen* and I paused, cupping my ears forward to catch more of it.

"She must meet him." And then something indistinct. A younger voice saying, "You promised me it was the last time." Something about no one else being ready. The younger voice was louder, but it sounded more like fear than anger. "One last time. And in return you let me go with them in the morning—to this place called Wilentelu." There was a long silence then and I nearly turned away to my bed, but then the voice came again, slowly as if nearly asleep. Brief and with an old, formal feel to it, but unmistakably a song of power.

"*Ada-gaom ebe-gyam; ebe-kael-gyam adye.* I am thy bones; be thou my skin."

Another voice then, saying, "Go fetch her."

I scampered back to the place they expected me to be, drew off the cat-skin, and did my best to pretend to be drowsing. Shortly, a voice called from the doorway, "Ashóli. Ashóli, wake up. The *byal-dónen* would speak with you."

I rose and followed, with my guide explaining, "He is old and has been ill. Do not spend his strength in mere pleasantries."

It was like a strange dream. They brought me into a small house, lit only by a pile of coals on the hearth. The old man sat wrapped in a heavy cloak patched together of all manner of skins, nodding as if in sleep. My guide touched his shoulder saying, "Ashóli is here to see you."

He stared at me without focusing; his hands clutched and stroked at the cloak he wore, as if he were working his craft. "Ashóli," he repeated and the word was slurred as if by drink. I was suddenly embarrassed, knowing they had wanted to hide this from me.

"*Byal-dónen*," I said, not having been given his name, "I wished to do my courtesy to you. I have seen your cloaks throughout the village and have rarely seen such fine work."

"Ashóli," he repeated again. "I thank you." And then, as if a curtain were drawn aside, his eyes focused and he truly *saw* me. Something flashed across that gaze briefly. Hope? Purpose? And then his eyes closed again and he shuddered.

My guide pulled me away. "Enough, let him rest."

I wanted to ask what his illness was. I wanted to know why he had no students to take the burden from him. I wanted... But I was a stranger as of yet, and I had already bullied them into revealing this weakness to me. I let it go.

In the morning when we had packed and saddled the horses, I pretended to be surprised when a young man was presented to me as a companion for our journey. A woman who I took for his mother presented him to me. "Daolesh has decided to bargain his services to your Marchalt. May he travel with you?"

I nodded, taking in the fox-fur cloak he wore. "Daolesh, can you ride?" I had seen a few horses around the village, but that was no guarantee among people more used to being, than using, beasts.

He ducked his head and said, "A little."

"Then we can share," I said, "and take turns in skin-form. Give Halkun your bag to carry and see if you can keep your balance back here." I patted the pad behind my saddle, hoping that the horse would behave.

He handed over a small sack of his things to be strapped on, made his goodbyes, put on his skin, and leapt to the horse's rump. There was a brief argument between the two of them as to his presence, but in the long run his lighter weight in skin-form would be carried easier than as a man.

With one or the other of us in skin-form while moving, I had few chances to ask the questions that puzzled me. Kers took it upon himself to begin teaching Daolesh more of the speech of Wilentelu when I was the one wearing fur behind the saddle, or taking briefly to the skies. That first evening I tried to draw him out, but on any question touching on the affairs of his clan he was silent and for the time I let it be.

Our return was swifter than our road out. How could it not be, given that we knew the way this time? Watching Daolesh, I remembered my thoughts the first time Eysla and I had topped the rise of one of the hills bordering the great river's valley and seen the green fields rolling endlessly into the distance. Wilentelu had a startling solidity, sitting where the river bent, as if the river itself had changed course around it. Daolesh exclaimed aloud when the city came in view, and we stopped a few minutes to rest the horses and let him look. From there on, he and I rode double in the human way and I told him an endless stream of things it would be useful for him to know in the city. More, perhaps, than I should have poured into him at one time. By the time we rode in through the gates he was stretched as tight as a cornered hare. "Don't worry," I assured him. "Remember that you're an invited guest. That means as much here as it does at home."

That reassurance was off the mark, as things came to pass. We went first to the Shalen. It was expected, though I would rather have returned straight to Eysla's arms. And we were expected—the word would have been passed as soon as we were seen riding down from the hills—but the welcome seemed a bit cold.

When we came before the Marchalt, he gave only the briefest of glances at Daolesh and asked, "Where is Eysla?"

The question made no sense and I stared at him.

"Two days ago she disappeared. From your house. From the city, for all I can tell. I wonder that—"

Fear loosened my tongue. "How can you have lost her? You have her watched when I'm away—we both know you do. Were your men asleep? What is the use of all your walls and gates if she can be taken from under your noses?"

He stayed me with a wave of his hand. "That answers my first question. But for the second, who might have taken her, and why?"

All I could think was that our home might hold some clue, and with nothing that passed for asking permission I strode from the hall, trailing the remainder of our party in my wake.

The house seemed untouched, with no more disorder than if she had stepped out for a moment. I went first to the chest in the bedroom where she stored her skin-cloak. Eysla wasn't yet enough of a Kaltaoven that she wore it everywhere, but if she had left with a purpose—word from her brother perhaps?—surely she would have taken it. No, the horse-skin lay folded neatly as it always did. And then I saw the carved token laid on the covers of the bed and snatched it up. It would have meant little to the Marchalt's men.

"What is it?" one asked.

I turned instead to Daolesh, demanding fiercely, "Do you know this?"

"It's a *gelkov*," he said uncertainly.

"No, do you *know* it? Do you know who made it? Why it was left here?"

He shook his head mutely.

I turned to the others and explained, "It's a trading token. The message can be read as 'You have something I want; I have something you want.' Whoever left it, they took Eysla."

"And what of this boy?" the Marchalt asked. "Is this about him?"

I shook my head. "I don't know how it could be. We saw him take leave of his kin. There was no secret about it and no complaints." Only that strange night-time argument. "Search our bags," I demanded quickly. "I swear we came away with nothing that wasn't honest trade."

The baggage had been left back in the Shalen, so it was back there again in a crowd and then everything was dumped in a heap on the floor. There were the usual bits of clothing, remnants of travel food, tools and trinkets, and from the bottom of Daolesh's sack, a small tied-up bundle of leather.

He cried out when he saw it. "No! No, I swear I didn't... I wouldn't..."

I heard terror in his voice, but the Marchalt's men heard guilt and seized him fast.

"This is what they think I took?" I asked him.

Daolesh nodded. "It must be. But I swear..."

"Don't swear me any oaths," I snapped. "Just tell me how it comes to be among your things if you didn't put it there. Was this a trap for you? For me? Was it meant to poison the Marchalt's bargaining?" I paused for a moment to explain for the others when Daolesh had no answers for me.

"What is it?" the Marchalt asked curiously. "One of your magic cloaks, I assume."

I bent and picked it up and nearly dropped it again. The leather was smooth and buttery-soft, but like nothing I had handled before. And as I touched it, the power trapped within it reached out to meet me, like a whispering or muttering in my head. I untied the knots and shook it free. A short cape, just enough to drape around the shoulders. A thing of power, definitely, but strange—and wrong somehow. Daolesh had recognized it, but when I brought it close, he struggled against the hands holding him and clearly feared to touch it.

"What type of skin is this?" I demanded. "Who wears it? Why is it important to you?"

"*Nalyev*," he whispered. "It is *nalyev*." And that was as much as I could get.

Once again, I translated for the others. "It is...I don't know a good word for it. A secret? A mystery? Something it isn't appropriate to speak of, not to strangers. He is—" I tried to think of a way to explain that would make sense in this place. "—under a vow not to speak of it." I looked the Marchalt in the eye. "You could force him, but I think it would mean the end of your plans among his people." He scowled, but nodded.

I was far less satisfied and turned back to Daolesh. "This is no longer a private matter for your clan. Someone has made it our business as well. They have taken my *kólvyashen* and I will do what I must to get her back." I wadded up the cloak and stuffed it roughly back into the empty sack and took some pleasure to see him flinch at the handling.

"Ashóli." The Marchalt was back in a mood to command. I knew it sat ill on him to deal in matters he had little power over. "Ashóli, this isn't king's business. I will do what I can, but it won't go as far as sending armed soldiers after these people."

"No need," I said. "They *want* to bargain."

"Is that why they came here and took her? Why they didn't simply go after you in the wilds?"

That brought me back enough to smile. "You're learning more about us than I thought. Yes, better an elaborately-staged bargain than a simple demand. It's our custom." I thought hard for a moment. "They won't be far away. Unless they have a skin-singer with them, they can't carry her inside someone else's skin against her will. And to get here so soon before us, the ones who came must all be wearing feathers."

The Marchalt picked up the trail of my thoughts. "So they can't have carried her off any further than humans can carry an unwilling captive. No horses have gone missing, of that I'm certain."

I frowned, trying to imagine myself in their place. "Not within the walls, I think. Too confined, and too unfamiliar—although at least one will have been a regular visitor here. They knew where to go and what Eysla meant to me."

"Will they have been watching for you to return?"

I thought of soaring high over the river valley on falcon's wings and nodded. "If we ride out of the gates, they will find us."

I was not as confident as I sounded, but it all made sense. They wanted a trade, not a feud. And I wanted Eysla back, not revenge. But I also wanted to understand what had happened. And that skin... Something about it gnawed at me. Laaki's stories had told of people who worked evil magic—not Kaltaoven, different kinds of power-working. If this skin-cloak hadn't been of Kaltaoven make, I would have thought it might belong in those stories. That made me tempted to cheat on the bargaining. Or at least to try. So before we went out of the city, I took a small thing—a very small thing—from the skins I had worked, and borrowed the use of one of the Marchalt's scribes.

There were seven of us who went out for the bargaining. The Marchalt changed his mind at the last moment and stayed behind. I think he felt his rank was not well served if he could only stand by and watch. But he sent not only the two men who had traveled with me, but another pair to keep watch over Daolesh and one whose duty was only to carry the skin-cloak and not let anyone take it by force or trickery. They were armed, but only with swords and knives, not with anything that might threaten a Kaltaoven in bird-skin at a distance.

The guess that they would be close by was only partly true. We rode out the gates and down the road towards the river landing at a slow pace, looking carefully in all directions. But the sign came from above, in the form of a raven that circled three times over our heads and then soared south following the river bank two hours ride to where the land grew marshy and grown over with willows. To come this far they must have stolen a boat, but that would have been easier than stealing horses. There were only three that came out to meet us, all in feathers as I'd guessed, but none wore a raven cloak and Eysla wasn't there, so I knew there must be more in hiding.

"I don't see that you have anything to trade," I began, breaking several of the rules of the game. "Until I see Eysla and take her hand, we have nothing to discuss." And for our side, I nodded to the man carrying the sack who pulled out the skin-cloak for them to see then put it away again.

They couldn't have expected to begin so one-sided, which gave the advantage to me. I suspected that I had another advantage: I was certain both Daolesh and I were innocent of the theft. There was more waiting and Eysla was brought forth from the screen of willows. The man who wore the raven cloak was Laeno, who had a bear's skin when I had seen him last—the man I had seen once in Wilentelu. This was important enough that someone had lent him both skin and song to speed ahead of us.

Eysla hadn't been taken easily. I could see bruises, and they had her hands tied before her and kept one hand on the rope. And her appearance was heralded by a stream of curses that were wasted on her captors as the only ones she knew that were strong enough were in her cradle-tongue. But she was sound and whole and she shouted when she saw me.

I pushed past them to greet her, giving no one a chance to forbid it. I took her bound hands and kissed her cheek. And as I slipped that small furred something into her curled fingers I said, "It's not quite as bad as that time your brother locked us in the store room, is it?"

She was completely bewildered for a moment, then closed her fingers tightly around the tiny pelt and smiled. "No, not quite that bad. But I'm not sure I remember how you got us out of that place."

"Try your best," I said, completing the confusion for anyone who was listening.

Custom demanded that we sit, and so we spread our cloaks and sat with the damp from the river rising around us. Custom demanded that those who had offered to bargain begin, and so I waited, which was a hard thing. Laeno took the lead. He wasn't the eldest of those present, but I thought all this may have been his plan; certainly his knowledge must have been behind it.

"*Byal-dónen*," he began, giving me the title that courtesy demanded. "Ashóli, since you have no patience for the old ways, perhaps we can finish this quickly. You have something of ours; we have something of yours. The trade is even. What do you say?"

"This was never an even bargain," I countered. "You know what Eysla is to me—the one to whom I've bound my heart. I know nothing of what this skin is to you."

"You don't need to know, except that we value it."

I interrupted, as if I found what he had to say of little importance, "And you have taken pains—and caused pain, I see—to steal away something of mine, but I never took your property. I have it now, but I did not take it. Look to those around you and ask who put it in Daolesh's baggage. He never took it, and neither did I."

"Liar!" one of the others cried.

From where he sat behind me, I heard Daolesh answer, "No!" before he was hushed.

"This is no ordinary skin-cloak," I continued. "When I know what it is, then we can begin bargaining for it." I stood and began walking away, leaving the rest in my party to scramble after. I half expected to be called back but the call didn't come.

It was well after dusk when we came again to the walls of Wilentelu, with one gate left open waiting for our return. My body and heart were both exhausted. I had succeeded in giving Eysla a possible key to her prison, if she could learn a skin-song from writing rather than speech. But I was no closer to solving the riddle of the skin. Was it foolish to believe something was wrong and that it was my task to fix it? Had I gotten too much in the habit of solving other people's difficulties? The Marchalt asked me much the same thing when we reported our failure to him.

"Maybe I'm wrong," I admitted, "but maybe this skin came into my hands for a reason. I can't think of any profit that would come to anyone from all this trouble. Maybe I'm supposed to solve the riddle."

"If what you want is to know what sort of skin it is, why not just put it on?" the Marchalt asked. "You say you can wear any skin you choose."

It was a simple enough answer. I can't say I hadn't thought of it, but that wrongness worried me. I took the cloak out of the bag and shook it loose. Daolesh made a strangled noise. No one had thought to do anything else with him, so he was still dragged willy-nilly into all our councils. "One last chance," I told him. "Is there something I should know?" He shook his head—not in answer but in refusal. With a sudden motion I threw the cloak around my shoulders and reached out to take on the spirit within it.

Through a fog, I could feel myself falling to hands and knees. But they were still knees, and still hands. My mouth moved, and another's voice came from it saying, "Be as quick as you can. The knife is sharp, and I am a dead man already." Then pain, like a fire wrapped all around me, and a voice chanting words of power. I flung the skin from me and heard screaming in my own voice.

The pain remained crawling all under my skin, but faded slowly. When I opened my eyes, I saw the high ceiling beams of the great hall of the Shalen. And the Marchalt kneeling beside me with a stricken look.

"Emeen," he said. "You put the cloak on and you turned into Emeen. He looked just as he did twenty years past, but that can't be. He was an old man. By now he must be—"

"Dead," I finished, struggling to sit up. "Dead. But not before *that* was cut from him." I pointed where I had thrown the crumpled wad of leather.

I heard oaths and curses from many of those standing nearby, and the one of the Marchalt's men who had carried the sack and handled the cloak started scrubbing his hands against the fabric of his clothing. I leaned on the Marchalt's arm to rise and staggered over to Daolesh. "What have you done? Do you know what they did to him?"

The haunted look in his eyes was answer enough but he said simply, "I've worn that skin. I and others before me. They have to drug us first, so we can bear the pain. But not so much that he can't work."

Things started falling into place, but still I asked, "Why?"

He shrugged, but it was more a gesture of despair. "He is our *byal-dónen*."

Telling some part seemed to have freed him to tell all.

"I was too young to remember when it happened, but we all know the story. Our luck turned bad and then worse. Three students he had trained over the years to make skin-songs and all had died: one from a fever, one attacked by a beast, one in childbirth. Then he fell ill with a growth gnawing on his insides. This—" He gestured at the skin-cloak. "—was his answer. A way to preserve his skills for us to use. But only he could make the skin-song, and he could only make it while he still lived. I don't think he knew..." Daolesh's voice had dropped to a cracked whisper. "They say... They say that he put the knife in his own brother's hand. And they say that the day after, his brother put on feathers and rose out of sight and then fell back to earth as a man."

After that, no one spoke for a long time.

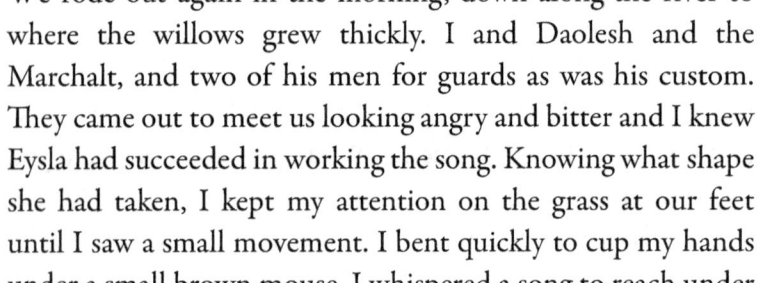

We rode out again in the morning, down along the river to where the willows grew thickly. I and Daolesh and the Marchalt, and two of his men for guards as was his custom. They came out to meet us looking angry and bitter and I knew Eysla had succeeded in working the song. Knowing what shape she had taken, I kept my attention on the grass at our feet until I saw a small movement. I bent quickly to cup my hands under a small brown mouse. I whispered a song to reach under the skin and then it was Eysla who filled my hands and arms. I kissed her proudly before pushing her back towards the Marchalt's waiting men and turning to bargain.

"I did not steal your skin-cloak, it stole itself." I waited until the denials and accusations had faded before I continued. "And it is with the cloak that you must make your bargain." With a shuddering breath I unwrapped the cloak and put it again around my shoulders. It was much harder this time, knowing what would come, but I knew why I had been chosen. I sang the song I had overheard that night in the village, "*I am thy bones; be thou my skin.*"

The fire wrapped around me again and I heard a voice crying out, "Forgive me! Forgive me, but let me die!" And when I could bear it no more, I shed the skin and stood gasping as if I had run seven miles.

When the roaring in my ears faded, I could hear birds singing in the willows, so quiet everyone had become. "Let him go," I echoed.

"We had no choice," Laeno said quietly.

"You have plenty of choices!" I shouted. "You are not the only Kaltaoven in the world. He was not the only *byal-dónen*. Is this what we come to when we hide in our villages and fear to speak to each other in the marketplace? You could have a dozen children with the skill to craft skin-songs and you would never know it because you cling to this...this sad abomination. My own clan wasted a generation doling out second-hand skins. Why do we never *talk* to each other!"

I had heard Eysla behind me translating my words for the Marchalt and the others, and as if summoned he now came forward with one of the Kaltaoven phrases he had mastered, "*Geol-dón pen-deah*. I would make a bargain."

I walked away to cool my anger and heard him distantly speaking of making Wilentelu a meeting place for all Kaltaoven. Of sending word out and bringing people together. Teachers, traders, skin-singers, suitors. And there would be work for those who chose to take it on. I remembered what he had said to me that day in his garden, *If I could have two of these people in every company of soldiers...* And I wondered what might be set in motion today.

After a time, Laeno came to me where I stood apart. "Is it something that can be done?" He seemed unsure what to ask. "To...to release him from the skin?"

"I can try, if that's what you choose." I was growing ashamed of my earlier words.

"We didn't choose this," he protested. "Amyen chose his own path."

I wanted to ask whether Daolesh and the others had made their own choices to wear the old *byal-dónen*'s skin. But perhaps they had, given the choices they knew. "I can try," I repeated.

They brought me Amyen's skin-cloak and I sat holding it in my lap. There was a part of the death-song that we sang when skinning a beast for a cloak that bade farewell to its spirit. And there were songs for funerals, for sending human spirits on their journey. I took the part of a skin-song that bound the power into the skin and turned it inside out, then braided the three together. As I sang it, I could feel unseen things loosening inside the cloak. It only needed one last push. I whispered, "*Lyev-gaal adye*, it's time to go," and the cloak crumbled to dust between my fingers. A breeze lifted the dust of Amyen and scattered it across the grove and up until it disappeared against the sky.

Hide-Bound

The Marchalt of Wilentelu had taken it into his mind to marry. That was why I was freezing on a mountainside looking for ravens. I scanned the ridge above the tree line and hugged my cloak of wildcat skin closer for warmth. It would have been warmer to wear it in truth—to put on the cat's shape against the cold—but I needed human eyes for this task. The rocky slope was still. Stiller than I'd grown used to through my years in Wilentelu. Stiller even than the village of my girlhood where laughing cataracts tumbled down the mountain canyons. Above the faint roar of the wind breathing through the pines I could hear Maaljan panting softly at my feet. No need for him to brave the chill without fur. A soft whine signaled his impatience, then he turned his head away, abashed that the wolf's voice leaked past human control.

I kept my gaze on the ridge, pretending not to notice. He was young. How Laaki would laugh to hear me say that! My teacher had despaired at my own impatience and arrogance. But perhaps that experience gave me more patience now. A speck of black arced slowly into view over the edge of the mountain then disappeared. I waited. Again it appeared, tracing a slow spiral against the wind rising up the slope. A singleton? I held my breath then let it out slowly as a second speck came into view. "Not here," I said aloud. "We have time to move farther up the valley before dusk."

Maaljan took that as a signal to shed the wolf's skin and rise to stand beside me. "How much farther, Ashóli?"

I knew he wasn't asking only about today's distance. "I need two more pelts. As far as it takes."

"There's two up there," he said with a scowl, nodding toward the ridge.

"A nesting pair. There should be plenty of this year's fledging to take instead. Ones too young to have mated and have territories of their own yet." Ones that had only half a chance of surviving their first winter. It's a bargain we make with the mute beasts: that we won't hunt them entirely from their homes or treat their sacrifice lightly. We hold a bargain sacred and that trust was already strained by the choice to take four.

I picked up the sack at my feet—the only burden I carried on this hunt. The dark, glossy pelts called to me from within, only half-sung to life again. One would have been enough to take on feathers. I had changed with a single mouse-skin once, when there was need. But the Marchalt had asked for a good show. *Do you have a raven cloak in that magic chest of yours?* It could take years to wear a new pelt into full size and the Marchalt had determined to marry in the summer to come.

Maaljan ran ahead to find dinner while I worked my way along the edge of the tree line where the ground was clear. The pair of ravens circled overhead, their eyes following me until I was well clear of their territory. We fed that night on a fat marmot: wolf and wildcat tearing it between them until nothing was left but skin. Then we slept together, fur to fur for warmth, to wait for the morning's hunt.

We caught the last two ravens on the third day after that. I sang their sprits to quietude as I prepared the skins, using sinew to sew all four into a broad collar that would fall over my shoulders down to the bend of the elbow. Maaljan watched in silent fascination as I worked. It couldn't have been the first time he had seen a new skin-cloak made, but we *byal-dónen* each have our own ways.

His own cloak was the gift of my teacher Laaki. I recognized the intricate, repetitive workings of her songs. But her skin-songs might have been the only ones he'd heard before the Marchalt's gathering-in coaxed the far-spread Kaltaoven villages on this side of the southern mountains to settle in the Wilen valley.

Those villages had been too far spread. In times barely in memory we skin-wearers—we Kaltaoven—had come out of the east to find homes in these middle-lands that were still thinly settled. In the old lands we had been hounded by the fear and jealousies of men. Laaki had known that for herself. I was only a girl when she came fleeing west from beyond the stone-built cities of Karskar where men still hunted us in the same way we hunted beasts. But in long generations of safety we had lost our way. We'd scattered too far, grown too secretive. Both kinship ties and knowledge grew thin. I had grown up amid the despair and in-fighting that could come when a village had no one to sing new skins for their children and skin-cloaks became a hoarded treasure. Other clans had turned to darker answers. No clan should risk the chance that no one would be born with the skills to become a *byal-dónen*, a singer of skins. Or that such a one might be born with no one to teach her.

And so I had delivered word of the Marchalt's bargain as far as wings could take me: a place to live in peace with men, to renew the bonds of distant kinship between the Kaltaoven clans and to forge new ones, to bargain more widely for our children's future and make certain that new singers would be taught. And—on the other side of the bargain—to serve the Marchalt in ways beyond what human bodies could offer. And now the Marchalt of Wilentelu had set his mind on marriage and I was to serve him in a raven's skin.

Maaljan had bargained to accompany me on this hunt in exchange for a skin-cloak for his sister's babe. A triple bargain: the most sacred in binding Kaltaoven together. He gave me his service, I sang a cloak for the child, and the sister pledged him a carpet and a set of bed furnishings to put aside for the day he made a separate home.

A red-banded kite, they wanted for the child. Swift wings and sharp eyes. It had changed us—this in-gathering. Where once we would have waited for a shape to call to us, now there was always the thought, *What can I offer; what value will this body bring?* It made me uneasy sometimes. The Marchalt kept to a bargain, but he was not Kaltaoven and his desires were not our own. And now what he desired was a bride.

I wove my song through the dark feathers and placed them around my shoulders, feeling the skin sink into my own as my bones turned in my flesh to embrace it. The forest changed around me, flatter and with more colors. The ravens' thoughts whispered in my mind and I sang them back to rest. In time they would embrace their dreaming. Eysla, my lover, said she still spoke with the spirit of the mare whose skin I had sung around her and I shivered from thinking of it. She had not been born Kaltaoven and refused to think it ill-luck to share her skin twin-minded to a beast.

I cocked my head sideways to check the space above me and hopped into the air. I had worn feathers many times before but each shape took learning again. I could see Maaljan leaping excitedly below and echoed his joyous yelp with a croak. It was well done.

We slept one more night on the mountain. The edge of winter was already sweeping in but we huddled with our furs only wrapped around us in order to talk.

"Why a raven?" Maaljan asked.

I thought how much to tell him: what I knew and what I guessed. "Because the Marchalt asked for a raven. He wishes to send messengers to woo a bride, and he wanted a raven among them."

There was so much left unsaid. It had been no surprise to anyone when whispers went around the city of the Marchalt's plans. When a man of his age is established and secure in his rule, it's past time to be thinking of heirs and a legacy. Well past time, for the Marchalt was no high-born noble to pass his power on to a son by blood. It was not for me to tell the man's secrets, but Maaljan knew little of the history of Wilentelu. What did kings and cities matter to Kaltaoven living scattered across the wilderness? He had only lived in Wilentelu for three years and had never seen the king during his circuit, still less his palace far to the south in the great city of Mergenel.

"The marchalts govern at the king's pleasure," I explained. "They rule in his name in far-flung lands newly come under the king's peace. If the Marchalt wants a son to take up that governance, the boy will need time to grow to manhood and prove himself. The Marchalt has spent years setting a strong hand on the lands along the Wilen, but those years were lost to a boy's growing. It's past time for him to marry."

There was more I didn't say. A wary king might think twice before confirming such a son. Two generations were as good as a title, they said. But Wilentelu was a long distance from the king beyond the mountains—a long distance to see into the minds of men who had carried his laws into the new *talodeshi* and who had become accustomed to their own power. A long distance to answer a challenge from a man who had found other allies.

Do you have a raven cloak? In the southlands, ravens were thought a carrion bird. But farther to the north it was said they set the raven on their banners and carved it on their house-posts alongside the sea-wolf and the great white bear. To the north ruled the *yallans*: princelings who had set out claims around the edges of the northern sea and bowed their heads to no king, though they might nod to each other. And the *yallans* had daughters.

I had known none of this when Eysla and I first came to Wilentelu, selling the horses that her people raised in the high hills. But years in the Marchalt's service had taught me much of the world. Carrying his messages taught me more. If I were given to wagers—and if such a wager were not a betrayal of his secrets—I would have laid silver on the guess that the Marchalt would be looking north for a bride, and sending me there in the spring. North, wearing a raven's skin.

When we returned to Wilentelu, I went first to find Eysla in the marketplace by the east gate where she was haggling over a contract with the chief of the carpenters' guild. Our booth there had grown since the days it was a bare space and we had lived by selling intricate works in wood and metal traded from distant Kaltaoven villages. Now others had taken on those trades and Eysla kept the contracts for skin-work and made bargains for those who didn't care to make their own.

It was the city-dwellers' way to make much of things written down, and so we set bargains in ink now rather than trusting to the memory of words. For our part, it was good to track what the fair price was for a letter carried, for the guarding of herds and travelers, for the finding of things lost beyond human senses and reach. These were skills we hadn't known to value until sold to men who lacked them.

I waited while Eysla spelled out the fees for fancy carving to the round, curly-haired man who stood before her.

"By the piece or by the day? Oseon is busy for the next month, so you can't have her unless you wait. Or you can hire her son for the rough work and wait to have it finished."

"It's madness to charge so much and still have to wait a month for some damned rat to chew on my cupboard."

"You know what a man with a chisel would charge," Eysla pointed out. "Skill is skill, whatever name you give it." Men like the chief carpenter were why Eysla was kept busy as a go-between. They might value our skills, but value was not always respect. She folded her arms and let him finish his bluster until they came to a meeting point. "Have the contract drawn and bring it tomorrow to sign," she instructed.

When he had gone, Eysla came to my arms. "I've missed you so."

"You say that every time, whether it was a week or a month," I answered, but I treasured the welcome. How long would I be away come the spring, when I went north? *If* I went north.

"And have you another cloak for your collection?"

I opened the sack to show her the sable feathers within. "I had to go farther than I thought, but it was worth the miles."

"A different skin for each day of the month," she teased.

She had only the one, of course: the horsehide cloak I'd sung for her when we first met. Laaki had thought me foolish to make a skin-cloak for one not born Kaltaoven. Foolish I had been, but I had never regretted it. And if Eysla had any regrets about casting herself into the chasm between her people and mine, she kept them to herself.

Most Kaltaoven had only the one skin. Only *byal-dónen*, skin-singers like me, gathered them up like treasure. Treasure to spend, to bargain with, and for me, most often, to use on the Marchalt's errands.

There were hours yet before dusk closed the market and I had a report to make. I left my cat-skin with Eysla rather than carrying it inwardly and put on the raven feathers to meet with the Marchalt. To make a good show. He enjoyed that sort of thing, so I took to the air and circled the Shalen—the king's house where he spoke in the king's name and dealt the king's laws—croaking loudly before landing before the guards at the door. I cocked my head at them and croaked once more. They were used enough to my comings and goings that they grinned and pretended not to find it strange.

"He's hearing pleas," one said and nodded toward the doorway.

I dipped my head in thanks and took to the air again, brushing the walls of the corridor with my wingtips until I came out into the vast interior of the Shalen. An army could be marshaled within that hall—or a people protected. Though from the stories I'd heard, even in the early years when the Marchalt's power was sometimes challenged it had never come to that. The city walls had been enough.

At my entrance he looked up from his chair of office—a plain one, not the ornately carved seat beside him that represented the king—and called out "Ha!" He raised his wrist as if I were a hunting hawk. It humored him, and so I came as if to his call and settled carefully, calling out three times before hopping down to take human form.

The men he had been speaking with stared at me. They must be strangers to Wilentelu, or they'd be more accustomed to us. I had learned to put on courtly graces in the Marchalt's service, so I bowed to them and said, "Pardon for my intrusion." They might have been no more startled if the raven had spoken.

The Marchalt waved them away. "I grant what you ask. See my steward and he will arrange things. So, Ashóli, are you ready for your next task?"

I cocked my head to one side as if I still wore feathers. "Surely not until spring?" He'd never said as much, but it had been easy enough to guess his plans. Winter would stop most travel except along the Wilen itself.

His look was sharp but he grinned. "There is much to be done before spring. I'll send a man to you. I want you to learn his tongue." I nodded and turned to leave. The Marchalt's orders were rarely more elaborate than that. But he called me back. "Ashóli, I've heard that ravens can be taught to utter human speech. See if it can be done."

The stranger came to me in the marketplace the next day, where I kept company with Eysla to make up for my absence past and that to come. If I'd had any doubts about where the Marchalt's thoughts had turned, the stranger would have settled them, with his straw-colored hair and sun-reddened skin. "Your lord says I am to teach you," he said awkwardly in something that was close to the traders' tongue heard in the market.

I nodded. He fingered the fringe of black feathers that lay across my shoulders and I suffered the touch. Perhaps in his land it was not rudeness.

"They say you are—" He reached for a word our common space failed to contain. "You are *volek*."

I couldn't know whether the name was true, so for answer I sang the raven's song aloud and drew the skin about me. Through the twist of the change I heard what must have been an oath. When I cocked my head to look up, he had stepped back, wide-eyed, and was clutching an amulet hung at his neck. At my back I could feel Eysla's sudden wariness, in case he should do more than swear, and I cast off the feathers to face him again. "I am Kaltaoven," I said, though the word would have no more meaning for him than his for me. "You will teach me your speech, as the Marchalt says. Come after the midday meal and name the world for me."

When he had left, Eysla chided, "You should not have teased him so."

I shook my head. "There is truth in what a man does when startled. That's a truth I couldn't have later." Whatever else we might have said to each other must wait, for Maaljan appeared, calling a greeting, with his sister's family in tow. We had guests to entertain.

The triple bargain had been fixed from the moment I had chanted *gyel-dón a-don*, but it was a custom to mark the fulfillment and there was a skin to be delivered, though it would be years before the babe could sing her own song. I spoke the formula to quit Maaljan of his service and he, in turn acknowledged his sister's payment. I fetched the cloak of ruddy kite-feathers from the chest where it waited and wrapped it around the laughing infant like a swaddling gown. I whispered the words of her song so softly that only she and I could hear, and then I commanded, "Wear thy skin!" and the feathers sank into her flesh for the first time.

An unfledged hawk is a comical sight, though no more so than a human babe, and no less beloved in a mother's eyes. She nestled the chick to her breast until it began to shriek in hunger. Is a newborn child ever anything but sleeping or hungry? Then I spoke the words to draw off the cloak and returned them both. "Is the bargain good?" I asked.

"*Gyel-dón a-don*," she echoed.

I would teach her mother the song. A guard in case... Many things might happen in the Marchalt's service. No need to court fate by naming them. But that could come tomorrow. Now was time for all of us to dine.

In the easy hour when food was set aside and before the day's work began again, I watched Eysla dandling the baby, making the small cooing noises that all mothers speak. How old had her own child been when it had died? I could no longer remember, if she had told me. That had been before we met—been why we met. They had blamed her for the child's death. Her husband's kin had whispered, and more than whispered, of sorcery and she had fled for her life. That flight had taken her into my path and later into my arms.

"Do you long for a child?" I asked when the others had left. I'd seen that look on her face before and had never dared to ask.

"Yes," she said. "I feared the bearing, but there is an empty place in me where that babe should have been."

It would have wounded me more if she had lied. In casting her fate with me, she had left that possibility behind, though we never calculated costs at the time. I had never made the same choice. There was a time when a *byal-dónen* would have been expected to stand aside from all bonds of affection. No more. There are too few of us. And how much had that custom brought on the thinning of our blood? But since I met Eysla, I had always known in my heart that I would never bear children of my own body.

"Yes," she repeated. "But if it were meant to be, the southern wind would have blown one to me."

It was a saying of her people and I couldn't help smiling at the vision of a squalling babe being floated over the hills on a raincloud, though we both knew better how children were made. She smiled back and we spoke no more about it.

Throughout the winter I spent every afternoon in company with the northerner—Laofi, he was called. At first we would wander the city as he pointed and named everything we encountered. I took curious note of the omissions and hesitations. He knew no words for wine or oranges, and the water-mill brought only an excitement that would not translate. We built the words together, and by the turning of the year I thought I could manage to babble like a child. Halkun, the Marchalt's steward, was learning too, and one more of his men. In time, we came together, laughing our way toward fair conversation as Laofi told us of his home. And in the evenings, I would sing my feathers around me and croak out the day's lessons for Eysla until she knew them as well as I did and the raven could pronounce them near as well as the woman.

The year turned and the sun climbed again. I could see the white fading on the distant mountains when I flew high over the city. As crops began to green the hills along the Wilen, my thoughts turned toward the long journey north and I held Eysla more closely every night though we never spoke of it. We lived well from my duties to the Marchalt, however often they took me from her side.

The Marchalt called us together at last—those of us who had been set to learn the northern speech—and he gave us our task. There was scarcely a need. Laofi had told us all we needed, though he couldn't have known. The Yallan of Dál had a daughter, fair and tall, of an age for marriage. And Dál lay nearest of the northern lands to our own, across the mountains and beyond the dark Bradwood. If the roads the traders took were strengthened between us, it would join the resources of the northern sea to the riches of the south. Messages had been exchanged and Ya' Saryu of Dál had invited the emissaries of the master of Wilentelu to bring his gifts and offers. It would be our task to turn those offers into a returning bride.

"Choose ten soldiers," the Marchalt told his steward. "Steady men who can keep their tempers, to keep watch and tend the horses." And then he turned to me. "Ashóli, choose four or five of your people to go. I leave it to you, but—"

"Make a good show?" I finished for him and he nodded. I followed his intent. One skin-changer was a wonder. Five in company was an alliance. It was part of the coin the Marchalt had to offer to an ally.

"Stay a moment," he added when the others were dismissed, beckoning me closer for private speech. "Halkun has my authority. He will speak to Ya' Saryu in my name. But you—" He was a man used to command. A thing that could not be made an order did not come easily to his tongue. "You make bargains. I have seen you talk a way through walls and over gates. Be my voice to the *yallan*'s daughter. I cannot give you authority in my name, but do what you can to bring her to me."

"I make good bargains, as you say," I answered. "And since I am to take a company of Kaltaoven with me, let Eysla be one of the company." The thought had been in my mind since he first spoke of it.

He grinned—a toothy grin that had nothing yet of agreement, only challenge. "And how would that be to my good?"

"Do you still feel the need for a hostage to ensure my return?" I asked. It might have been wise when I first took service with him, but the gathering-in of the Kaltaoven had erased the need for that anchor. "You send a company of soldiers, of men. If the *yallan*'s daughter returns with us she will want the company of women. More women than only me."

"You could choose another."

I counted on my fingers. "I will ask Maaljan, who leaves no obligations at this time, and old Laeno who wears a bear's skin. There is no other of that shape who would go. Given what Laofi has told us, I think it would be well to ask one who sings to the boar, and for that shape only a man will do. And my cousin Soeghe who has run for you as a hound. But I can think of no other woman who is both free to go and would serve the purpose. And—" I could not tell if he wavered. "—Eysla too has been learning the northern tongue. She can add to my persuasions."

"Very well, choose whoever you will," he said with a wave of the hand. "Only bring me my bride."

In another month it would have taken only two weeks travel to come within sight of Ya' Saryu's lands. But though spring had come to the valleys, there was still snow enough in the passes to send us east out along the road that led on at length toward Karskar. We would not go more than an eighth of that distance, but only until the mountains settled low enough to cross easily. Returning along the far side of the peaks, we kept to the higher wooded ground as long as we could, for when the track finally descended through the Bradwood toward the coast there were two days of picking our way along a hurdled path across the open bog—a path too uncertain of footing to ride and too exposed to view for the soldiers' comfort. The wetlands explained much of why these lands had gone unsettled still.

Despite the presence of that log-built road and the signs of traders' camps where the land rose briefly above the damp, we began to doubt our goal until the great north sea came into sight. At first there was only the occasional glint of silver from the top of a rise, then a thin line that that stretched across the horizon, peeking over a narrow shingled beach along the water's edge. The trackway led to a spot of higher ground, past a few empty timber shelters and a fenced enclosure of close-cropped marsh grass, and ended in a long stone jetty, leading out into the lapping water. It was clearly a place where others had waited for passage in the past, though there were no boats to be seen at the moment.

At Halkun's request, I took to the air and soared high above to make sure of our way. Before we'd come to the shore, I had thought to see something like the lake at Dyelenol, but larger: a vast expanse of open water reaching perhaps farther than I could see. Instead, from above, it seemed more like a ploughed field after the rain, with a broad furrow on the near side, arching out of sight to either end, and chains and sprays of islands scattered along the far edge, nearly hiding the shore. When my eyes followed the stone finger of the jetty pointing across the water, I could make out pale towers peeking above the wooded islands. That would be Ya' Saryu's fortress.

Halkun heard my report and squinted to measure the afternoon sun. Two of the soldiers had collected what dry wood could be found along the shore for a fire and the horses had been turned out to graze. "Take the Marchalt's message across now," he told me. "We'll have time to make ready before you return." There was grumbling from the soldiers at the lack of rest, but he silenced them with a word and set them to cleaning and polishing their gear. My company began their own preparations as I once more sang feathers about me and set off across the final stage of our journey.

I could feel the vastness of the water beneath me. The flight was short enough but the spirits of the ravens whispered to me uneasily, knowing there would be no rest until I'd crossed. White gulls glided below me and plunged into the water, shrieking and quarreling over their catch. Once I saw dark shadows pass below, then crest the waters with a plume of breath before disappearing again. They were the sea-wolves that Laofi had said claimed a tithe of men when angered. From above, the maze of islands slipped away and the fortress tower rose as a beacon. The *yallan's* court stood at the water's edge, rising from a rocky outcrop, with the sea lapping its base and the town sprawled out behind it, barely contained by low timbered walls.

They had word of our coming, of course. I could see a sharp-eyed watchman in the highest tower looking out over the water. The smoke of our fires would have been signal enough. But they had no word of the nature of our coming. No chance for rumor to run ahead. *A good show.*

I neared those towers from high above, searching for the best place to settle and making time to draw the eyes of those below by the shape of my flight. I wanted a crowd as witness. But more than that, I wanted to make certain of my welcome. The men of the north revered the raven in spirit, but ravens rarely neared the haunts of men. An archer might think to try his hand against such a tempting and unnatural target. I soared slowly, ever lower, croaking as first one, two, then more looked up and pointed. The wind whistled through my pinions as I circled, always turning with the sun for luck, though that became harder as the stone walls teased the air currents into knots.

The raven's eyes could pick out individual figures now and I looked for the dance of movements that would tell me their lord had been summoned to see the wonder. There: ripples in the pattern of men. I was uncertain at first; there were several places where attention pooled, like stones in the river's flow. As I dropped below the level of the peaked tower roofs, I set my sights on a tall, dark-haired man who stood on the steps before the hall with others ranged about him not by chance.

At his side stood a woman, his equal in height. I might have thought her his lady except that her head was bare and her hair braided loose. Her gown was the deep blue of the sea and her hair the yellow of wheat. On her fist she held a snow-white gyrfalcon, hooded and quiet beneath her stroking hand. I knew that I was seeing the Marchalt's intended bride. And I knew then that she would not be an easy heart to win. The look in her eye matched what I imagined lay beneath the falcon's hood.

There was a covered well in the courtyard before the steps and its roof would put me at a level with those standing by the hall doors. So I settled myself on the peak of the roof and croaked loudly three times, ready for flight if need came.

Silence fell, broken only by the whine and yelp of a dog. The faces around me held fear or awe or perhaps something of both. Praying that all my practice would serve, I turned my voice to human speech. "Greetings, to the Yallan of Dál!" I called, facing toward the woman. I could see no one standing near her of an age to be her father. Disbelief flickered in the people's eyes, thinking their minds had deceived them. "Greetings," I repeated, "from the Marchalt of Wilentelu." Now I could see comprehension. "The Marchalt sends his messengers to treat with you. They wait on the far shore for you to receive them and grant them leave to cross." And to provide us with ships, of course, for we had none of our own.

The man at the door to the hall stepped forward, still amazed into silence. The *yallan*? Surely he was too young, but he seemed to think my greeting addressed to him. There was some mystery here. The tall woman at his side laid her hand on his arm, and said, "Noble brother, shall you not go welcome our guests?"

We had feared that the *yallan*'s dignity might require that he wait our crossing. That would have upset our plans. But the marvel of a raven's greeting and invitation was sufficient. They were swift to take ships, the long oars sending them skimming over the water. I flew ahead to warn the camp to be ready, then returned to circle the small fleet as it crossed.

We had practiced our welcome so often I had forgotten how it might look to a stranger—and I could never guess at how an ordinary man might see us. When the *yallan*'s ship was docked at the jetty and the other ships beached and all the men gathered on the shore, Halkun urged his mount into view from between the huts. He rode with no saddle or bridle. Even for show, Eysla would not suffer those and she had never before given the favor of bearing anyone but me. Behind Halkun, the men on foot came into view, brightly dressed and carrying spears—because it was what men did—but wearing no other arms, to show the peace of their intent. Only then did the Kaltaoven move forward: a sleek brindled hound and a wolf, slipping through the ranks of the men as if between trees. A bristled boar snorting and pawing at Eysla's feet. Then a sable-pelted bear pushing through on her other side and rising up to tower beside the men. I could hear the surprised cries and murmurs from the northerners below me as we emerged, one by one, to take our places in the ranks. The *yallan* stood his ground, though some of his followers looked back toward the ships.

When Halkun raised his arm in greeting it was my sign and I dropped from the skies to settle on his raised hand. At that signal, Eysla reared as if in battle and he slid easily and lightly to the ground while all we Kaltaoven shed our skins as one and stood as men and women among the ranks. Our cloaks of fur and feather glinted with new golden clasps, set with gems. *A good show.* We had learned the value of proud display, living so closely now among humans.

I had seen too much in my travels to be certain of our reception, but it seemed the Marchalt had calculated the outcome correctly. There was shock and wonder but our numbers were too few for fear. And the ruler of Dál was on his own ground with more men around him than we numbered. I would have liked to see the lady's reaction but she waited on the far shore. If she were to be lady of Wilentelu, best to know soon what she would think of us. But this was a time for men to talk. Halkun went forward alone to give his greetings and letters and receive the *yallan*'s welcome in the Marchalt's name.

We gathered our things, leaving the horses to look to themselves with the promise of grooms left to watch them, and we boarded the ships to cross over. I took Halkun's suggestion and folded myself in my raven-cloak again, chanting just enough of the raven's skin-song to catch the northerners' ears. I flew above the ship, looking down into the water, but this time saw no trace of the dark sleek shapes I'd glimpsed before.

When the ships disembarked at the wharves, I settled myself on Halkun's shoulder, drawing sidelong glances from the *yallan*'s men. I still wanted to make my test. We passed in by the water-gate through the walls then across the yard into the hall where the lady waited. Before the muttered whispers of those who had brought us over could reach her ears, I launched myself from the steward's shoulder and changed in mid-air, dropping lightly into a bow before the blue-gowned woman. With the cloak of feathers swirling around me, I held her eye, my head cocked slightly to one side as the raven's had been and I saw nothing in her gaze to give me pause. For the benefit of all who watched, I repeated my message from before. "Lady of Dál, I bring you greetings from the Marchalt of Wilentelu."

No start of fear, no cry of delight, and no sign that this was the first she had ever met a Kaltaoven, though I doubted we'd ever strayed this far north. She gave a regal nod and I backed away to take my place among the party.

It was someone else at the side of the hall who started and gasped loudly enough to catch my attention: a pale, slight woman with hair like the fall of night, and so swollen with child that her time must be near. She took a step toward us, but a man seized her by the arm and spoke sharply in her ear. When I turned back to the *yallan*'s daughter, her expression had turned to distaste—perhaps something stronger—but not toward me. She, too, had turned her gaze to the pregnant woman. Another story to be unraveled.

They feasted us that night with the Marchalt's steward sitting at the *yallan*'s right hand and the rest of us ranged among the lower tables. When the man next to me on the benches had conquered his unease with a mug of ale, his tongue loosened enough to settle the mysteries I had seen.

The old *yallan* had died. That much I had guessed. A sudden apoplexy, a mercifully brief lingering in his bed, and then the gathering of powerful neighbors for the funeral. And that was when the arrangements had unraveled.

There had been no contract with the Marchalt, only the invitation to send emissaries. No one had questioned the old man's plans for his daughter Brida's marriage when he lived. But now it seemed there were two more rival suitors.

Only his father's pledged word had kept the new lord of Dál from bowing to their pressure. His sister's marriage had become not merely the seeking out of new ties and bonds but the balancing of a sudden shift in power. Ya' Sarfrad was young and untried and there were those who wished to stand in the place of an advisor to him as he found his feet. What better stake for this advisor to have than as brother-in-law?

The visitors had come with the excuse of paying respects and most had left, seeing the lay of the land and seeing who would vie for that land. But two had stayed. The younger man I thought of little moment—a stripling, eager but untried—until I learned he was the younger son of the Yallan of Esulon. Younger sons had been known on occasion to become eldest sons. The world was unchancy. But he was so little regarded that I never heard him named other than Esulon's son.

The other seemed a more solid rival: Waithas, the Yallan of Forrag. A man in his prime with thick sandy hair and a close-clipped beard. A neighbor, whose lands would be said to border on Dál to the west, if it weren't that water everywhere separated them. Watching him I could guess why the old *yallan* might have passed him over. They must have been close in age: a consideration not so much for his daughter's youth but from seeing the man too close a rival. He moved with confident assurance and stared closely at us, weighing and measuring. A strange smile played at the corners of his mouth when he looked at me, as if he knew some secret he thought would set all our show at naught.

Watching him, the second mystery was solved as well. The drink came out in great pitchers and the Yallan of Forrag gestured to the small dark woman I had seen before. When she came forward, moving awkwardly, to pour his cup, I once more saw Brida's eyes flick to her in distaste.

"And who is that?" I whispered to my seatmate.

He spat over his shoulder into the rushes on the floor and then looked round guiltily as if worried he'd been seen. "Nuulo. She's nothing—a wild islander. Forrag brings his leman here into the hall where he would court our lady. And she must swallow the insult for the sake of good neighbors."

I began to think the Marchalt might have done better to bring his own suit here. This would be no simple treaty. My neighbor's talk turned to questions and I spun tales of the south that I knew he would pass to his fellows before the morn. But my eyes followed Brida, thinking of my task.

To the Marchalt she had only ever been Dál's daughter; even her name had been new to me. She seemed as calm and regal as the crowned ladies I had seen in Mergenel. I did not know yet whether that was her true nature or perhaps a skin she put on for strangers. What had she thought of her father's plans? Would her brother's decisions have the same weight?

When the welcomes had been finished and the dinner cleared, we went outside the walls to the tents and pavilions that had been raised for us. The excuse made was that the visitors lingering from the funeral had filled all the rooms within the walls and in the town as well. I could not be sorry that we would have open air around and above us, even though the honor might be less. Eysla and I claimed a chamber to ourselves—a measure of privacy we gained for being the only women of our company.

I had no time to enjoy it, for Halkun came saying, "Ya' Sarfrad will see me in the morning and I will discover how badly our plans have gone awry." He, too, had learned the bones of what we faced, though he'd learned it from the man himself. "Tonight I thought you might find a few corners where sharp ears could do us a good turn."

He meant ears sharper than a woman's of course. I pondered what shape would serve me best. Hounds wandered freely in and out through the hall and I might borrow my cousin's cloak to mingle with them, but there were places a dog couldn't easily go, and who could tell but that his shape might be recognized now. Sneaking in corners would best be done by something small that the people here had not seen us wear. It would not yet occur to them to be wary of chance-met creatures. I fingered the scrap of mouse skin that had served me well in the past. That was perilous. The halls were prowled by fierce and feral cats and I didn't care to have my disguise lost to save my life. But those cats gave me my answer.

My favorite skin—the one I had inherited from my grandmother—had come from a forest cat far to the south and east. Among the granaries of Wilentelu, that shape would have stood out for its size and length of fur and the tufted tips of the ears. Here it would be otherwise among beasts that might have wild blood themselves. They slipped in and out at the kitchen door looking like small lynxes. I outmatched them only slightly in weight. And for that reason, as well, the hounds in the hall were accustomed to leaving them in peace.

There were so many secrets I wanted to sniff out, so many places to listen. Kitchens were always good for gossip and I might pretend to be no more than what I seemed, but the rough accents there were beyond what I could master. I padded my way through the shadowed corridors toward the private chambers back behind the hall where the *yallan* might be found. I followed the sound of raised voices, past a curtain and squeezed through a carved screen. It was Ya' Sarfrad and his sister. I found it difficult to follow the thread of their argument through the anger in her voice and his low whispers and I crept closer.

"In the hall before me! How dare he!" Brida's voice came sharply.

"You should know better than to take notice," her brother soothed.

"It's an insult to you and a shame to me that he flaunts her before my face. Is he so certain of your favor?"

Then the young *yallan*'s voice again, "The islander woman means nothing. And the only shame is that you demean yourself to take notice. Of course he has a woman. What did you think? That he came an innocent boy to court you? Our father had his bastards and you will learn to deal with your husband's the same. He only wants a bit of managing. Don't ruin your chances from the start by being a scold."

"My chances? You haven't yet convinced me to consider him, much less to accept him."

"Have you changed your mind? You weren't so eager for this...this *Marchalt* before."

Her voice came back less hotly. "No, I wasn't eager. And that was before we knew he trafficked in sorcery. But Father wanted the southern alliance. His reasons were sound."

"Father is dead and I am Yallan of Dál now, not you. I'll do what I must to keep this place safe."

There were footsteps then and I backed farther into the shadows under a bench as her skirts brushed past me. At the door she turned. "If you and Waithas want this alliance so badly, then tell him he must send the woman away. Tell him I want no sight of her face or her belly within my hall."

"No, Brida," he said.

And then she was through the door, slamming it behind her. He lingered there, trapping me in my hiding place as he called a servant to him and demanded ale. By the time I was able to slip away unnoticed to report to Halkun, the hall was empty except for snoring men and a lone late-scavenging hound. It seemed little enough to tell. He knew already that we had a harder task before us than we'd thought.

Eysla awaited me in the small canvas shelter we'd claimed. The straw pallet nearly filled it entirely and a thick featherbed barely fought back the chill of a northern night. I took on my cat-skin again to curl closely at Eysla's side until her hands stroking me drew me back to human form for the touch of skin on skin and the comforts found there.

I woke early from the strangeness of the sounds and smells and slipped from the bed carefully so as not to disturb Eysla's sleep. She always had the knack of finding rest wherever we were. The *yallan* had told us to be free and welcome in his lands but Halkun had been more cautious, telling us to stay clear of the village that sprawled out on the landward side of the fortress. Instead I went to walk along the water's edge, picking my way past the stone quay.

Only the larger ships were there. Out among the islands I could see fishing boats dotting the water. There had been a great deal of fish at dinner the evening before. I thought about those dark shapes I'd seen in the strait in my crossing. The fishermen seemed unconcerned, but what hazards waited in those waters? Once I came past the quay, the walls of the fortress rose straight up from the sea, with small waves lapping rhythmically against their base in a way that told of deep waters and sharp cliffs. No enemy would come this way. It was said the walls of Wilentelu had guarded against attack when the king first claimed the valley. But I had never known them as anything more than a line keeping the chaos of the town from spilling out into the fertile fields. This place spoke more loudly of enemies fended off. No windows but narrow slits, and the walls topped with deep crenellations where men with bows might lean out. And whose ships might those archers aim for? I looked back at the small fleet that Ya' Waithas had brought. It seemed a great force for a funeral visit.

When I could go no farther along the narrow walk just above the water's line, I scanned up along the face of the stone and there, almost directly above me, a pale face leaned out from the top of the walls, gazing over the water. It was Waithas' woman. Her dark hair formed a cloud as she combed it with slow inattentive strokes and braided it into order. She had the look of a woman alone and though I had no warrant from Halkun to seek her out, I told myself that she might let slip a word or two that we could use. Surely she would be set against this marriage for her own reasons?

I drew the raven feathers around me. The wind that met the stone face lifted me easily. I circled twice, thrice, up to the level where she kept watch then slipped around to hover unsteadily a few steps away until I could drop onto the top of one of the crenellations. She showed no surprise; she must have seen me soaring up the currents. From the look of wary recognition, I was certain she knew me from yesterday. She spoke but so softly the wind whipped the words away before I could even tell which tongue she used. When I cocked my head to listen better, her voice was more urgent—a bubbling, musical tongue that wasn't the northern speech I knew.

The words pulled and tugged at my mind as if I should have known them. I shook my head and hopped down to the narrow walkway within the walls to shed my skin. The croaking raven's voice might serve for portents but not for ordinary conversation.

She seemed struck dumb. Her lips parted in the same expression I had seen before. I suffered her to reach out and touch my skin as if to assure herself of my solidity.

"Do you know us?" I asked.

"*Volek*," she said in the northern tongue. "Skin-wight." And then in that musical tongue she had first used, "*Tuvis*."

It was an old word from a time of legend and barely distinguishable in her strange accent. But I repeated it "*Tuvis*. Yes, *Kaltaoven-dón je-am*."

Her breath caught as in a sob. Before she could speak again, a voice called from the stair tower behind her. "Nuulo! Come away from there." The Yallan of Forrag looked daggers at me as I returned to feathers and perched on the stone wall before launching myself out into the upwelling wind.

Halkun was closeted with Ya' Sarfrad all day and when he returned late in the afternoon to our little camp his news looked to be less than good. We had obeyed him and kept to the castle grounds. The soldiers found such fellowship as men did without words in common, both with the *yallan*'s men and with the women in the yard. We Kaltaoven had kept together, still wary of what reception the ordinary folk might give us. But in the thin evening light after dinner was finished, we took to the open fields beside the town to show ourselves. Soeghe and Maaljan played touch-and-go under Eysla's feet as she ran in easy circles and I dipped and glided above her, now to one side, now the other. It was no more than childish play but we could see a line of watchers staring at us and only returning to their work as we returned to camp, one by one shedding our skins in their view.

In the last few years we'd lost some of the wariness that had haunted us so long. The people of Wilentelu scarcely took note when we moved among them now. There we had worked to seem ordinary. Here our task was to remain strange and mysterious, yet it was a public strangeness that left me uneasy from the scrutiny. Brida had come out to watch with Esulon's son at one hand and Forrag at the other. As we returned breathless and laughing from our sport, she signaled her women to give us drink—sweet honeyed ale that cloyed on the tongue rather than quenching thirst—and asked in that careful clipped voice she used with all her guests. "Do you ever ride to the hunt? Or to war with the Marchalt?" Her questions seemed no more than idle curiosity but the two men beside her listened closely.

"Not to war, Lady" I replied. "The Marchalt has not needed our services there. There have been no true battles in the lands around Wilentelu in the time I've served him. But we enjoy the hunt as much as any."

"How is it that you serve your master," she asked, "if not in war?"

I would have argued the name "master" except that I hadn't the words to better explain our bargain. "In many ways," I began. "As swift messengers. To carry small objects quickly. Those who wear feathers have helped to map the Marchalt's lands. But we bargain with the folk of Wilentelu for many things. Some large, some small. There is a woman who chose the shape of a squirrel and is a woodcarver. She makes intricate designs with her teeth. And Maaljan who wears the wolf-skin hires himself out to guard newborn lambs in spring. There are many tasks we do better than those who have only one skin."

"And the pretty filly?" Ya' Waithas said as we stood talking. "What would she cost?"

I couldn't afford to give offense though his tone would have raised fur, had I worn it. "Eysla doesn't trade in her own labor," I told him. "She makes the bargains for others and records the contracts. She is what you might call a merchant of work." He frowned and shrugged. The question had not raised my esteem for him.

"We ride out hunting tomorrow," Brida said. "Perhaps you would like to join us?"

Her gesture included all our party but I answered, "For myself, I accept. And my cousin Soeghe loves to run with the horses. But I must ask the others." Maaljan did not care to hunt in human form and we had already learned the northern hounds would not abide his presence. Few Kaltaoven were at ease on horseback but I added, "Eysla, I think, would enjoy the ride."

"You do not ride her yourself?" Ya' Waithas asked.

"No," I said with as much patience as I could master. It wasn't the truth, for Eysla had offered me that service many times when we traveled together. He wouldn't understand that difference.

I had looked for the dark-haired woman throughout the day: in the hall, at dinner, and now when the crowds gathered to watch our sport. She was keeping herself hidden, though whether from Waithas' displeasure or Brida's I didn't know. And she was not on the parapet the next dawn.

My mind worried over what she had said like a hound over a bone. My ears might have played tricks, I told Eysla. And yet...

Eysla chided me at last, "Have patience. You're certain to see her somewhere. It's not so large a place that she can hide forever."

Halkun urged me again to listen everywhere I could. He was beginning to fear a long siege with no good end. Ya' Sarfrad looked to his neighbor and saw little use in a southern alliance when his own concerns stood closer. Today I would listen to those who rode to the hunt while Halkun was again closeted with the *yallan*.

I might have guessed that we would hunt with falcons, having seen Brida's fondness for the fierce bird she'd carried at our first meeting. We rode up the valley to a long clear lake where geese dotted the waters and herons stalked along the marshy shore. Eysla grumbled at the short-legged shaggy creatures we rode, so different from the elegant hill-running horses her own people bred. Our steeds picked their way slowly along narrow trampled paths while the hounds ranged out in their first exuberance, flushing lake-hens from the reeds. Not until we had come out to a broad shrubby meadow was there space for me to come alongside Brida closely enough for speech.

"What prey does your falcon take?" I asked, thinking the bird a safe topic to draw her out.

"Duck and heron, perhaps, but wood pigeons are more likely," she answered. "She took a goose once, but it was only by luck. If we start a hare, she might try for it. Will you—" She hesitated and looked at me curiously. "Will you be flying today?"

I had worn my raven-cloak, of course—for show—but I shook my head and laughed. "I wouldn't care to come under her talons! And a raven's hunting would make poor sport to watch, I think. Will you take her with you when you marry?" It was not too soon to turn the conversation in that direction.

Her glance darted toward me again. "Perhaps. Do you hunt with falcons in Wilentelu?"

"Not I, though the Marchalt enjoys it when he can. And some of my people hunt in falcon-form."

Eysla added, "I've heard that around Mergenel they hunt with eagles."

I nodded. "I saw it once when I was traveling there on the Marchalt's business."

She fell silent and then her attention was claimed by young Esulon until we came to the edge of the open fields. The birds were cast off and sent up to wait while the hounds spread out more purposefully to find what they could flush. I watched Brida as her two suitors danced attendance, paying more mind to her than to the hunt. She showed neither favor nor disfavor, despite what I had heard the other night. The bile she had betrayed toward Ya' Waithas' woman was not loosed toward him. She was pleasant always, but cool and distant as if holding herself back until she knew which suitor her brother favored. How much would her own choice matter in the end? It must have some value or they would not court it. And that choice was my quarry to pursue as well.

When the others had ridden off to follow a wayward chase, I made excuses to tell her more of Wilentelu and of the respect I had for the Marchalt. Respect, but not quite liking. I guessed that she would value truth. He was a hard-edged man: always keeping to his word but unyielding in his purpose. I think the lady could tell that from my answers though she showed me the same cool face she had turned toward the others.

Only once could I see deeper, when she had called the gyrfalcon back to her hand while a huntsman gathered up the heron it had downed.

"She and I are alike," Brida said, stroking the bird's breast gently as it tore at the meat in her hand. "Wild creatures, tamed by habit and usage. I don't know if she even remembers that she can fly free."

"And yet you set her free every time you hunt her," I pointed out. "And she returns, because she chooses to. Where would you fly free if you chose?"

Her glance was sharper and unguarded this time. "You ask that? You who are the whistle calling me to your Marchalt's glove?"

"I bargained my service to him," I said carefully. "And I have found it a good bargain, for me and for my people. If I have sometimes worn jesses, I put them on knowingly." I looked over at Eysla. She had been my jesses at first, but it had been no burden. "I have flown free in my time. It's a wide world and perilous. I am content with my bargain."

I think she might have said more, but the others joined us again and she smiled and spoke them fair as before.

The islander woman was serving Ya' Waithas at dinner once more, though he kept her close and spoke sharply when she stared at me from across the hall. Eysla followed my gaze and leaned over to whisper in my ear, "She is near her time. I can tell by the way she carries. No more than a week, maybe two." And indeed, the woman paused in pouring to put a hand on her back and stretch as if always in discomfort.

I was still untangling the currents between these people. Had Brida left the matter alone for now? A frown creased her brow every time her attention turned to that end of the room. And as my eyes were on her, I saw her head jerk up before I heard the crash of crockery and a low cry. The pregnant woman was doubled over, leaning on the table where she stood, splashed with the spilt ale.

Brida's face still wore impatience for one long moment, but it was washed away by something else. Sympathy, perhaps, and then that queenly look that spoke of setting her own concerns aside for duty. She crossed the hall in a few swift steps and called out to two of the serving women as if the accident were nothing more than ordinary, "Frola, clean up this mess. Heri, take her up to my chambers."

The Yallan of Forrag began to protest but she stilled him with one sharp reproof.

"This is women's business. Have you no eyes to see?" There was nothing he could say to that. Did he fear for his leman's safety in Brida's hands or only that she would be out of his power for a time?

I thought no more of the matter until we returned to our camp for the long evening twilight and one of Brida's women came to seek me out. "My lady begs you come. That foreign woman is asking for you and says she will not rest until she speaks with you."

The summons had been for me but Eysla stuck closely by my side as the woman took us back through the corridors and up into the private women's chambers in the south tower overlooking the sea.

I had never ventured to these rooms in my evening prowling. They were brighter than the hall below—not in light, for the fires on the hearths and a handful of rushlights lit the room barely more than what seeped in through the narrow shuttered windows. But there were colorful tapestries on the walls and half-finished needlework set aside where the firelight was best. Along the edge of the room was a jumbled chaos of sleeping cabinets and truckle beds, spread with checkered blankets and furs. Brida's falcon stood on a perch in one corner of the room, fluttering restlessly from the unaccustomed activity.

The women were gathered into the alcove formed by the jutting out of the round tower, where one of the truckle beds had been set apart behind a screen. The islander stood in their midst, protesting and pleading until she saw me enter. There was not the bustle and noise I would expect at a birth. Brida crossed to where we waited in the doorway.

I asked, "Is she...?"

"Still days to wait, or so they tell me," she said. "It often comes this way for a first child, they say." Her mouth twisted in rueful concern. "But best to get her out of the hands of men, and that man in particular. It will be easier on her. To make her pour at table in her condition!"

Brida led us to the alcove, shooing the others away and saying, "Nuulo, I've brought you the raven-woman as you asked. Now will you rest?"

The islander's face was drawn, either with pain or worry, and I could see her hands shaking. There was a stone bench built into the wall where a window cut through. Uncertain what to do, I drew her down to sit beside me and took her hand. Eysla, more practically, knelt and began rubbing her feet, muttering, "Do none of these women know what a bearing mother needs?"

Nuulo looked warily at Brida, and then across the wide room to where the other women gathered out of earshot. But when it was clear the lady herself had no plans to leave, she began speaking. It was hard to understand her at first. The music of that incomprehensible liquid tongue mixed with the northern speech. "I can't wait," she said urgently. "He's coming." There was more that I couldn't understand. "I must have it back. You understand. Help me!" Her voice held a frantic edge.

"Women have borne babies before," I soothed. "They'll know what to do." I felt at a loss, for I'd never done more than watch at a birth.

"No," she protested. "I must have it! I must have it now! I can't wait." Her voice was wild and she kept looking fearfully at Brida.

"She's made no sense at all since we brought her up here," Brida said sharply. "See if you can calm her enough to rest."

It made no sense to Brida, but there was a conversation Nuulo and I had left unfinished. "You called me *tuvis*," I said. "Where did you learn that word?"

Again, the wary glance toward Brida. "They mustn't know. They won't... Promise me!"

Brida made an impatient noise but said, "I'll keep your secrets, woman. Say your piece."

"I heard it from my mother," she said at last. "And she from her mother and so on back to the old days when we came out of the east. That was what we called ourselves before we lost our songs. Now we are only the Mora, the sea people."

My breath caught at what she seemed to imply. Was this another long-lost clan that might be gathered in? "What songs did you lose?" I asked, dancing around the question between us.

"We lost our songs," she repeated. "But not our skins. But I...I lost that too. He took it from me."

A look of pain came over her. Eysla laid a hand on Nuulo's belly but she brushed it off.

As if it were an ordinary thing, I asked, "What skin did you wear?"

"The gray seal, of course," she said. "As we all do."

She looked up as Brida hissed a word sharply between her teeth. From the corner of my eye I saw her make the gesture that Laofi had made when he first saw me change.

"There was never a need to resent me," Nuulo told her. "I could never have the place in his life that you seek."

"And Ya' Waithas took your skin?" I asked.

I think the horror must have shown in my face for she quickly said, "Only to keep me with him. He's kept it safe, he says. He promised me. And someday..." But then she touched her belly again and began to cry. "But now I can't wait. I must have my skin back before the child comes."

It was a long tale and strange that she whispered to us, her eyes darting fearfully to the cluster of women at the far side of the room.

The Mora had been Kaltaoven once, or something like to us. Long ago they had traveled along the islands and the rifts from the east, seeking better lands—or better seas. From their legends we must have been more similar then. Then, they had worn many forms, but as they traveled, more and more they took to the creatures of the sea: the great wide-ranging gulls, the seals, the ice-bears that swim from island to island, and other creatures of the deep whose names were strange to me.

In time they lost their songs, she said. Perhaps it had been what we feared: with too few singers, it's easy to lose the skill. But they had found another way. I listened torn between curiosity and unease. If they bore their children in beast form, they could renew each generation's skins, with the babes changing and shifting in their mothers' arms until they came to wills of their own.

It seemed unthinkable. Who would have dared to try such a thing the first time, risking the chance that the babe might never be more than beast? Yet it had become their life. The clans had sorted out by the shape they favored and drifted apart from each other. The gulls she thought had swept on to the west. The ice-bears had been hunted to their deaths. Nuulo's people had settled in the scattered northern isles where they made cozy homes deep in the sea caves along the shore, safe from the visiting fisherfolk by the very barrenness of the land.

But still they ventured out and walked among men to trade and take common cause against the sea. Sometimes it happened that a man or woman of her people would take a human lover, leaving the isles for a time to share a different life. And sometimes that human lover turned jealous of the sea.

"How could he do such a thing?" Eysla asked. But I could see her remembering. She knew how a man's love might turn sour.

"I loved him," Nuulo said with a sudden defiant look in Brida's direction. "And he loves me, in his fashion. But he is a man who holds fast to what he loves. Even if he might once have set me free, now that I bear his child..."

I think that was when Brida's heart turned completely toward her. I remembered what she had said during the hunt with that falcon-look in her eye. Her face was still grim but she seated herself on the edge of the truckle bed and took Nuulo's hand. "Would you have us steal the...the sealskin back for you?"

She shook her head miserably. "It isn't here. I searched through every trunk he brought. It's locked away back in Forrag."

"Ashóli could make—" Eysla looked up at me too late for any caution. Hope had already leapt in the seal-woman's eyes. "Ashóli could make you another."

"Make?" Brida asked.

"Perhaps," I cautioned. It was no use to keep secrets too closely now. "My people are not born to our shapes as Nuulo's are. I am *byal-dónen*—a maker of skin-cloaks. But I don't know if I could craft a skin-song in your tongue."

"You made one for me," Eysla said fiercely. "And I'm not even Kaltaoven."

My misgivings shrank before the hungry silence that fell between us four. "I can try, if you have something as *kalgeol* to trade for it." I used the ancient word, thinking it might be something we shared that far back: the sacred bargain that bound lives and kin together. It must be no mere market exchange, not when the making of such a skin was involved.

"I have nothing to bargain with," Nuulo said in despair.

But a new thought had come to me. The work I had been sent here for was always in my mind. I looked up at Brida. "You do have something. The lady of this place wants you gone, and that is a gift that you can give in exchange for the skin."

I explained what I could of our custom in the face of Brida's confusion. Her people had a reputation as keen traders; I thought she might understand.

"That would leave me in your debt," Brida said sharply.

I nodded. That was my intent.

"If I am brought into this bargain," she continued, "I should think I might have some say in it. And it matters nothing if she leaves. Ya' Waithas would only find another leman. That I accept as the way of men."

"Only if you accept his hand," I said. The choice was not entirely her own; we both knew that. But her word would still have weight.

She nodded.

I turned once more to Nuulo. "It would be a bargain of uncertainties. But if we swear to try, we can find the threads to bind it."

"But it must be now! Soon!" Nuulo said, smoothing her hand across her belly as if it twinged again. "Or else he will be lost to me—or I to the sea."

"I could..." I began, thinking it would be as easy to make two skins in a foreign tongue as one would be. But it was no answer. It would be years before the babe could use it—years when she would be tied to a human child and her escape once more postponed. "Then best I should be quick about it. Are you both content to settle the bargain after I return?"

I thought about what Halkun would say, for me to go haring off and all my work yet to do. But there was opportunity here. If I could catch Brida up in this net it might be our best hope of success.

"Now tell me," I asked Nuulo, "Where nearby can I hunt seals? And how will I tell the wild beasts from your own kin?"

It was hard to convince Halkun of the value of my errand and I had little time for it. I think he did not understand the worth of the webs that women weave out of sight of men. But I had the Marchalt's charge and now my own desire as well. The Marchalt might want alliance and power but I saw in Brida a good Lady for Wilentelu, with a strong mind to keep a hand on him and watch over us. I left Eysla at Nuulo's side, to be a companion to her in her travail as strangers both in this land.

The wild seals bred far to the north but it was late enough in their season that the young males would be ranging in these waters—those that had no mates to watch over. And it seemed I needn't risk sorting out beast from Mora on my own. They had followed her, watching over her, Nuulo said, since the time she first met with Ya' Waithas. She had seen them—her brothers and cousins—from the deck of Waithas' ship, streaking through the waters just out of sight unless you knew to look, following the boat's wake all the way from Forrag to this place. Never less than two, they watched over her, hoping for a chance to win her free. She had seen them in her walks upon the parapet, bobbing in the waters out where the fishermen launched.

I found them by the end of the second day, following sleek shape after shape until I spotted two that paralleled each other in ways that spoke of human minds. I couldn't tell if they had seen me. How often would a creature of the water look up into the sky? Perhaps they hadn't, for as dusk fell, they made no evasion as I followed them to the rocky shores of a small island midway in the strait.

If I'd been uncertain I had found my goal, that doubt was shed with my feather cloak when they answered my change by rising onto two feet themselves. They stared at me unspeaking with eyes as dark and bottomless as Nuulo's, and as full of sorrow. They were naked, the both of them, which startled me until I thought further. It was only natural that creatures born to their skins would not encompass clothing within their beast-forms. They poised for a moment with their skins in hand as if ready to fling them on again and throw themselves into the water.

I called out, "Nuulo sent me," and that stayed them. They asked how she fared and I told them as best I could of our plan and what I needed. They had less of the northern tongue than Nuulo did from her time among men. When they understood my intent, one stared at me in horror, the other—though troubled—nodded slowly.

"Yes, so it was done in the old legends. You will take a dead skin and make it live for her. Our forefathers must have done the same. But to betray the seal-kin..." He sounded doubtful.

"I wouldn't ask you to betray them," I said. "Only I must be certain the skin I take is from a beast and not by ill chance from one of your own kin." I left the thought hanging between us.

"No fear there," the horrified one said. "There's none but we two and my cousin in these waters."

The other added, "There's a colony that sleeps a few leagues farther north. I'll take you there—to be certain."

It was full dark when we reached that beach, but the moon gave enough light to see the silvery shapes lying close-packed in sleep. My companion turned to human form long enough to give a low soft call that was answered only by grunting bleats. "It is safe," he said. "Any of these." And then he turned back to the water and was gone.

I stood unmoving for what seemed like an hour, making my choice and thinking how best to do the deed. Were they unafraid of men or did I not count as a man? When I approached with my long knife in hand there was only the crunch of bodies turning in their sleep. I was afraid one strike might not accomplish the task but my aim was true.

Then came cries and a struggle and the sudden bolting of the pack for the safety of the water. We were left alone then, the seal and I. When the last twitches had stilled, I flayed the skin as neatly as I could and began the preparations. The edges of a song had begun to take shape in my mind but this was a new challenge. It might be days before I had shaped the proper words.

It is not our way to eat the bodies of the creatures who lend us their shapes but I'd brought no food with me and I prayed his spirit would forgive me when I changed to raven form and followed the ways of a raven with carrion. The rest of the seal-pack did not return.

The power of a skin song is not in the words themselves, but in the way those words bind skin to flesh. When I had made Eysla's skin-song in the traders' tongue, it had been out of pride and arrogance, never thinking that I might fail. I thought of composing Nuulo's song in my own Kaltaoven language but could she learn the words? And would they have power for her or be mere noise? I struggled with the strange tongue, feeling like a babbling child trying to express ideas far beyond me. Slowly I could feel the power take shape in my mouth and under my hands, weaving through the drying hide to make it soft and supple and hungry for the touch of skin.

On the third day, I took the sleek gray pelt and placed it over my shoulders, speaking the words only and not reaching out with my own inner power. It fell in place around me as I dropped to the shingled beach. I could smell the salt of the water like rich wine. The soft scraping lap of the waves on the stones called me to the sea. But this was no time to dally. I turned again to take up my wings and fold the sealskin within me to carry back to the fortress.

Every day that passed had torn at me. The two Mora men did not return and now I flew swiftly, without pausing to tell them of my success. I came to one of the windows of Brida's chambers and pecked on the rippled glass until a shadow fell across it and Eysla let me in.

Her face and the thin cry of an infant told me I'd come too late—too slow. Nuulo lay still in the truckle bed, looking tired and pale beyond what any new mother might. And at her side, swaddled in bright cloth, lay a red-faced child, still with the crumpled face of a newborn.

Three days. Everything can change in three days. The chamber was deserted except for we four, though I could hear voices drifting up the stair. I crossed to the bed and held out the sealskin but she turned her face away as if she couldn't bear to look.

"I spoke with your brother," I told her. "He showed me where to find them."

"It's too late." Her voice was bleak and hollow.

"It's never too late." I knelt down beside her and laid the seal-cloak across the coverlet. "Let me teach you the song. Try it."

She rolled away from me, rising from the bed and taking up the child when he began fretting and mewling. "You don't understand. He'll take this one, like he took the last. I have no way to hide it while the babe grows." She looked down at the bundled infant. "Can you give my son a skin as well? I won't leave him behind."

I had to shake my head. "Not yet. Not until he can speak the words." Nuulo was no *byal-dónen* to be able to wrap another's body within her skin-cloak. "Perhaps you could take—"

"Don't you see?" she said sharply. "Waithas knows he has a son. If he held so tightly to me, do you think he would let his child go?"

I was angry at her despair and held the cloak up to her once more. "A creature died to give you this. Will you set that sacrifice at nothing?"

Her mouth trembled. She reached out, longing. Eysla came over and took the babe from her arms so she could hold the cloak in both hands. Then—before I could speak the words of the skin-song for her—with a sound that was both a sob and a cry of triumph, she swirled the cloak about her shoulders and fell slowly to the floor, a curve of sleek gray fur and liquid dark eyes.

If I had known! Two days spent setting the song's power into the northern tongue when she could wear it without words! Was that time wasted? But perhaps the skin had needed my craft to make it ready. So much here to learn!

There came a sound of voices and footsteps up the stairs and I crouched beside her, urgently coaxing, "Come back. Let it go for now. They mustn't see you like this."

The skin peeled away and I helped her to the edge of the bed. She clutched it bundled to her breast where only moments before she had held the child.

I looked over my shoulder at the women who had come into the room and halted their chatter at seeing me. To Nuulo I said softly, "Will you bargain for the skin-cloak or return it to me and go your way?"

She made a mirror of her earlier gesture: holding the bundled skin cradled in her arm and reaching longingly toward the child that Eysla held.

"Forgive me, I can't. I can't give it up again." I saw the sea in her eyes: wild and changeable and stronger than any other love. It was the child she begged for forgiveness, not me.

Eysla saw it too. "Make him a part of the bargain," she urged. "Give him to Ashóli and take your freedom."

Nuulo was stunned as if she couldn't understand what had been offered. "What do you—"

My beloved looked at me with a reflection of Nuulo's longing in her eyes. "Ashóli, offer her the bargain."

I could see it then: the pieces all coming together. The balance and the web. From me to Nuulo to Brida and back. Only one piece was missing and for that I needed to know Brida's deepest desire.

I called to one of the women who had entered, "Could you ask your mistress to come speak with us?" She nodded and went off to fetch her. And when Brida returned she knew in a moment what was afoot and sent the other curious ears away.

I began the familiar lines to open the bargain-making, stumbling over the translation of them into the northern tongue.

A bargain, a bargain I see,
A bargain, a bargain we three,
A bargain, soon will be,

"Here is the triple bargain we will make," I said. "Nuulo, I will give you the sealskin cloak in exchange for your child. Is that a fair bargain?"

I could see her doubting and weighing. She protested, "But Waithas will never let him go, not to foreigners. Not to anyone."

"We will arrange it. Have no concern for that. Is the bargain a good one for you?"

She nodded and then said aloud. "It breaks my heart, but my heart is already broken. The pieces will be smaller, that is all. It's a fair bargain."

I turned to Brida. "And here is the bargain you two will make: that you will help Nuulo escape this place and swim free. And in exchange Nuulo will leave your hall as you desired and come no more between you and your suitors."

Brida shrugged. "It's a small enough thing; it seems fair to me."

"And there is the third bargain I would make to seal the pact." Here I was treading on shifting ground. "Brida, choose the Marchalt of Wilentelu to be your husband. And if you are able to convince your brother, then name the bargain that seems fair to you in exchange. So long as it is within my own gift to give, you will have what you ask."

Her eyes narrowed in consideration. "I am inclined to trust your judgement of Wilentelu's offer, but this seems rather a bargain I should make with the Marchalt himself," she pointed out drily.

"I cannot promise anything in his name, only my own," I said. "My service to him is to convince you to accept him. The rest is between him and me."

"A dangerous bargain you make then," she said. "How do you know what I might ask?"

I bowed my head in acknowledgment of the risk. "You would be lady over all of us in Wilentelu. If you will not be fair and just, best we should know it at the start." My words held not threat, but caution. She would be coming a stranger into our land and it was true: given such a choice, she would be judged on her wisdom in exercising it.

"And if I cannot persuade my brother?" she asked. "He favors Forrag, you know."

I smiled. I had seen another strand in the web of the bargain. "What will Ya' Waithas do when he sees his leman and his son escape his grasp after they were in your care?"

Understanding dawned. "He is unlikely to take it well."

I nodded. I was depending on him not taking it well.

Brida looked from Nuulo, to where Eysla held the babe, to me, and said, "There's no telling yet whether the bargain is fair, but I will take it and carry my end as it falls out."

I reached out my hands to the both of them and we joined in the web as I spoke the words that ended the ritual. "*Gyel-dón a-don*. And now," I said, "to plan the rest."

It had been the ease and speed with which Nuulo took on her seal-form that gave me the key. "Eysla do you recall that trick we played to convince your husband to let you go?"

She nodded. I remembered that wild chase along a mountain path, wearing her borrowed skin to lure the hunt. The horse's hooves thudding along the narrow rocky path. And then, just as the path turned, a leap out into the void. But what the pursuers hadn't seen was the winged form that flew out from underneath. All they saw was the horse falling into the ravine below. She smiled broadly, understanding what I intended, though the other two were puzzled.

"Here is my plan," I said. "It will be dangerous, Nuulo, but you would be free of him and the child will be safely beyond his concern."

The time was carefully chosen. Nuulo was to go walking on the seaward side of the castle walls in the morning, as her habit had been before. It would be early enough that fishermen were still setting forth and could bear witness along with the sentinels that stood watch on the towers. And so she was seen, moving slowly along the parapet, holding a tight-wrapped bundle close in her arms and gazing longingly out over the waters. She paused under the gaze of one of the guards and stepped up through the crenellation where the water swirled deeply at the foot of the wall. And then she cast herself out with a flutter and confusion of garments.

She fell in a long arc through the air. A woman's scream cut the morning stillness. The fishermen looked up; the guards on the walls looked down. But no one noticed that the shape that hit the water was sleek and gray-furred. It disappeared beneath the waves and was seen no more.

I do not know who took courage in his hands to bear the news to Ya' Waithas. Word spread quickly in the hall and the quiet morning hour turned to chaos. I contrived to be there as if by chance when he came raging in. Men held him back when he would have mounted the stairs to Brida's chamber, demanding redress for his son's death.

Brida was the model of concerned sorrow as she came down to meet his wrath. She offered soft words in exchange for his anger until the moment her brother appeared. Then her speech grew harder.

"Am I to be blamed," she asked, "if your leman prefers the caress of the rocks to your touch and the sea's bed to your own?"

I think he might have struck her then, save that the Yallan of Dál seized his wrist and spoke cold words of warning. In that moment our fate turned. It is easy for a man to look aside at how a comrade treats his woman. Harder to miss how he treats one's own sister.

I slipped from the hall unnoticed and went to tell Halkun that if he worked cautiously and swiftly his goal would be won. He had the upper hand in bargaining now.

And then I returned to the tent I shared with Eysla where she leaned over a basket that held a mother cat with three kittens. One of the three was larger than the others with the look of a wild forest cat.

She scooped the kitten up and cradled it against her cheek with deep contentment. "Take it off so I can hold him properly," she begged.

I shook my head. "Not until we're away from here. How could we explain a baby's crying?"

The negotiations dragged out for another week after the day the Yallan of Forrag ordered his men to the ships in anger and left. Esulon's son left more quietly a few days later but he could see which way the wind was blowing. Ya' Sarfrad could not be seen to agree too quickly, lest he lose his bargaining power, but this was a dance we all understood well. Halkun remained patient, Brida held to her bargain, and in the end the betrothal was made.

They decked the ships with banners and flowers for the brief trip, rowing across the straits to the mainland: a joyful farewell in place of a more formal delivery of the bride. Six of his men would accompany us back to Wilentelu along with the women who would come serve her in her new home.

I wondered what Brida's thoughts were as she stood there on the deck, still proud and regal with the white gyrfalcon on her wrist. She gazed, not back at home, but ahead to the far shore. Had she long since made peace with the fate of noble daughters? And what would she demand of me for the completion of the bargain?

We were out nearly to the middle of the channel, well away from even the furthest arrow's flight from the castle, when the other ships appeared. They bore down on us with the wind at their backs from among the maze of islands. An entire fleet could have lain hidden there. The air filled with shouts from the other Dál ships to either side. Ya' Sarfrad barked orders, but though every man wore his sword for show, this had been meant as a pleasure trip. The oarsmen bent more strongly to their task, but it was clear the other ships would overtake us long before we reached the far shore.

"Waithas," Brida said where she stood beside me. "He means to take by force what he could not have otherwise."

I could see no identifying sign on the ships but these people knew every plank and sail. He must have been waiting out of sight for just this chance. How long had he been prepared to wait? Or were there spies within Dál who had slipped away to warn him when the time came?

The men prepared to fight as best they could as the other ships neared us. Then the leadmost of Waithas' ships bobbled in the water like a child's toy and we heard shouts of fear across the distance. The second, as well, listed sideways then righted itself in confusion. And through the waves between us I saw enormous sleek black shapes cresting through the waters and disappearing below again: those mysterious dark forms that I had seen in the depths the first time I flew across these waters.

"*Marwa*!" a man cried, "Sea-wolf!" his voice rising in terror. Two shapes rose from the water beside the first of the Forrag ships, tilting it wildly. A man screamed and fell from the other side.

And now the attackers were among us, a confusion of wooden shapes and dark whales that somehow never touched Ya' Sarfrad's own vessels. We saw fear on the faces of Waithas' men as they drifted past, as if they had already slipped into the other world and knew themselves for ghosts. Even left untouched, our ships lurched violently in the roiling waters and Eysla and I grabbed for the rail to avoid being thrown to the deck. Brida's gyrfalcon was screaming and bating and she unhooded it and let it fly free to safety for the moment.

With a splintering of wood, two of the Forrag ships were driven together violently and began to sink. And still those great beasts rammed and rocked from below, always touching only our attackers.

I leaned over the rail to watch them go by and caught a flash of one small jet eye. I briefly wondered if there were a human mind behind that gaze but its flesh was not shaped for expression and then it was gone. And then, among those gleaming black forms, I saw a smaller gray-furred shape, dipping and gliding through the water beside them. A second joined the first. Now I understood. Nuulo had known better than most how loath Waithas would be to let a woman slip from his grasp.

The ships were close enough that we could see the faces of the Forrag men: their terror and frantic struggles, the two sinking ships with men clinging to the wreckage and a few—the bold ones who could swim—striking out for Sarfrad's second ship in hope of being rescued. I could see Waithas himself in the remaining vessel, his face contorted in anger as he realized his bid had failed. Our own ships soon won free of the chaos. Ya' Sarfrad urged the oarsmen to lean to again. With the danger past, Brida drew out a small lure and whistled sharply to the gyrfalcon, calling it back.

As in a dream, I saw what happened next. In the other ship, Waithas' head jerked at the sound of the whistle. He looked up and shouted something to one of his men and a bow was placed in his hand. Just as the falcon hung suspended ready to come to the call, he loosed an arrow and it fell, not gracefully but in a limp tumble into the sea.

Brida shrieked in rage and anguish but the deed was done.

It was a somber not a joyous company that came to the stone jetty and disembarked on the far shore. Two of three of the Forrag ships were lost and men in numbers as yet uncounted. But no mark was seen on the Dál vessels and not a man hurt.

As we stood, still amazed, there came a shout and a hand pointed toward the water. We turned to see three gray seals drawing out in the shallows of the stony beach. One humped forward then rose to become a woman. Nuulo came forward, carrying a small white bundle in her hands.

"You!" Ya' Sarfrad exclaimed in confusion.

But she addressed Brida. "A sad wedding gift," she said. "Not part of our bargain. We saw the ships waiting hidden in the channels and feared what he might do." She placed the small limp-feathered body in Brida's hands, offering, "I'm sorry. She was a noble creature." And then to me, "May I see him one last time?"

I went aside to where Eysla held the basket-cage and returned with the infant, now swaddled in a soft cat-skin. Nuulo's lips trembled and she traced a gentle finger along his cheek. I saw tears glistening in the corner of her eyes.

"Be good to him," she said. "And when he comes to the age for it, give him a form that loves water, if you can."

I thought of the river otters that played along the banks of the Wilen and nodded. "I will."

Then she turned and went to the water's edge. In a single fluid movement, she threw the cloak about her shoulders and dove into the waves and was gone.

The ceremonies of leave-taking were swallowed up by the bustle of packing, retrieving our horses from the grooms who had tended them, and arranging saddles and burdens. Of a sudden I could think of nothing I wanted more than to be on the road home. As Eysla and I stood apart from the work, Brida came to us, still carrying the feathered carcass.

"I listened," she began, "when you spoke with Nuulo about skin-songs and changing. And when your woman—" She nodded at Eysla. "—said that she was not born to your life."

I guessed what was coming next, but waited to see what she would ask.

"You owe me your part of the bargain," Brida said. "A fair bargain, if it is within your gift." She held out the bird. "Give me wings. Make me a falcon cloak to match your raven. Teach me to sing your songs. Let the Marchalt know that I will come to his wrist willingly if I am allowed to fly but I will not let this alliance be a cage or a leash. Can you do this?"

I thought of how I would answer to the Marchalt when he learned of my bargain, but it was by his command that I'd made it. *Do what you can to bring her to me.* And if he could take no joy in a wild falcon-bride, then he didn't deserve to have won her.

"Yes," I said. "*Gyel-dón a-don.* I will give you wings."

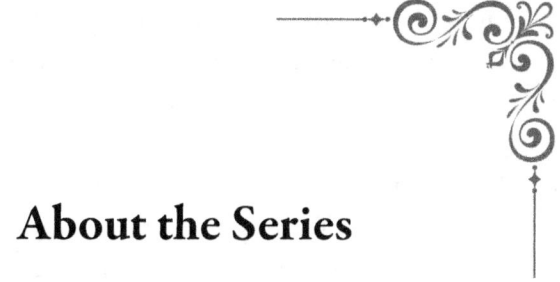

About the Series

"Skins" was my first professional fiction sale. The story came to me from a mixture of a poem I'd written about an owl shape-shifter and a dream about being chased in animal form. And because it was accepted for the *Sword and Sorceress* anthology series, I wrote another story the next year with the same characters, and it too was accepted. The progression of the overall "plot," such as it was, came from asking "and then what?" So the world just grew as my characters explored it.

Four stories came out for four years in a row. Then graduate school got more intense and I stepped away from writing fiction for a while. In 2003, with my PhD in hand, when the series was picked up under a new editor, I returned to Ashóli and Eysla's adventure. And after that volume, when the series again changed editors and also publishers, inspiration struck again.

But when I thought about the story that would bring the adventures of my shape-shifters to a natural conclusion, I realize that story would be far too long to meet the requirements of the anthology series. In fact, "Hide-Bound" just barely keeps to the limit for a novelette at 17,000 words. That was when I conceived the idea of gathering all the stories up in one place, topped off by that final story.

I may have briefly considered trying to pitch the collection to a publisher, but given the shape of my publishing career I decided the better idea was to use it to learn the ropes of self-publishing. The only problem was, my regular job (the one that paid the bills) took up too much of my time and energy to have much left for learning a new trade. And so the Skinsinger project waited for its time to come around. At my retirement, I opened the files once more, a full thirty years after "Skins" was published.

Because the series "just grew" and my ideas about the Kaltaoven and their world evolved across the series, I decided to do some light revisions of the previous stories to provide better continuity and consistency. Thus the versions of the first six stories are slightly different from what was published in *Sword and Sorceress*.

The perceptive reader may guess that I know far more about the Kaltaoven language than appears in the pages of this book. If there's enough interest, I just might blog about that on my website at alpennia.com[1].

Heather Rose Jones

1.　　http://alpennia.com

Don't miss out!

Visit the website below and you can sign up to receive emails whenever Heather Rose Jones publishes a new book. There's no charge and no obligation.

https://books2read.com/r/B-A-GAWGE-PIWRG

BOOKS 2 READ

Connecting independent readers to independent writers.

Also by Heather Rose Jones

Skinsinger: Tales of the Kaltaoven

Watch for more at alpennia.com.

About the Author

Heather Rose Jones is the author of the Alpennia historic fantasy series (from Bella Books) and the fairy-tale novella *The Language of Roses* (from Queen of Swords Press). She has sold short fiction to *Sword and Sorceress*, *Lace and Blade*, and *Podcastle*, among others. She has non-fiction publications on topics ranging from biotech to historic costume to naming practices. *Mother of Souls*, one of the Alpennia novels, was awarded the Gaylactic Spectrum Best Novel for 2016.

Heather creates the Lesbian Historic Motif Project blog and its associated podcast, presenting research on gender and sexuality in history as a resource for authors writing historic-based fiction, as well as promoting lesbian historical fiction in general.

Heather has a PhD from U.C. Berkeley in Linguistics, specializing in the semantics of Medieval Welsh prepositions. She has retired from being a discrepancy investigator in biotech pharmaceuticals.

Read more at alpennia.com.